BURNING LIES

GWYN BENNETT

Storm

To request permissions, contact the publisher at rights@stormpublishing.co

Ebook ISBN: 978-1-80508-375-7
Paperback ISBN: 978-1-80508-377-1

Cover design: Tash Webber
Cover images: Shutterstock, Unsplash

Published by Storm Publishing.
For further information, visit:
www.stormpublishing.co

ALSO BY GWYN BENNETT

ONE

The Silver Strollers were in full flow. They were nearly at the halfway point of the morning's walk and they'd managed to not only take in some great scenery, but also cover Tessa's knee op, the temporary closure of the local health centre due to a Legionella scare, and the appalling number of potholes in the town's roads which was the result of the council running out of budget. They'd just moved on to the latest report into the benefits of vitamin D, when the smell of smoke and charred wood interrupted the fresh flow of spring air.

There were seven of them, and they met every couple of weeks to go for a walk and to socialise. Usually they were eight, but Tessa had been having problems with her knee for some time and was now convalescing thanks to some keyhole surgery. Susanne was the route planner for the day – they each took it in turns. She'd taken them about twenty miles from town to the outskirts of Thistleford, a small village where they'd parked their cars and set off on a circular route around the countryside.

'Can you smell that?' Liz asked Susanne, looking around for the source of the burning.

'Yes. Probably a farmer getting rid of some rubbish or dead wood.'

'There's something odd about it...' Liz continued, sniffing at the air. 'I've got an excellent sense of smell you know.'

The pair slowed down, looking for the fire, allowing the rest of the group to catch up.

'What's the matter?' Nicky asked them, her eyes peering out from behind the thick glasses she always wore.

'Can't you smell that burning?' Liz said.

'Yes, but we're in the country; it's probably a farmer doing something.'

'That's what I said,' Susanne replied.

'But what if it's a fire and nobody knows about it. Someone could be in danger or it might burn down trees.'

Susanne gave an imperceptible sigh. Liz was well known for her overthinking of situations. 'It's fine, Liz – it's just a little bonfire, that's all. Come on, we need to get going if we're going to make it back to the village in time to get home for lunch.'

Liz pulled a face but followed the rest of the group down the country lane. Hedgerow and trees grew either side of it, making it difficult to see across the fields that surrounded them.

They'd been lucky with the weather. The forecast had threatened rain but thankfully there had been just one tiny shower and the pale spring sun was working hard to evaporate the shallow puddles along the lane, sending faint shimmers of water vapour rising up from the ground. The bushes and trees had started to show the first buds of the new growing season and the birds were in full-on courting mode, their song filling the air as they worked hard to impress a prospective partner. The English countryside was shrugging off its winter overcoat and getting ready for the warmth and heat of summer.

For a few moments, the smell of burnt wood in the air was forgotten as the Silver Strollers carried on their walk and returned to the subject of vitamins.

'What's that?'

Claire, Judy and Trish had taken the lead and come to a break in the hedgerow, where a metal gate led into a field. The others gathered around them, looking to where they stood staring, open-mouthed.

'It looks…' But Susanne didn't finish her sentence. What she was going to say was incredulous. Impossible.

The air around the women turned chilly.

'Let's get out of here,' Dee said to them, the look of fear on her face mirrored in their own.

'We can't… We can't just walk away. There's seven of us; we've all got mobile phones.'

As Susanne said it, several of them reached into their pockets and pulled out their handsets.

'I've got signal,' Liz observed, relieved.

'Me too. We should call the police,' Trish added.

'What if it's not real?'

'Real? I think we can all see it!' Liz said, her voice rising a couple of octaves.

'You know what I mean. It could be a dummy.'

'It's horrific,' Nicky whispered. 'Who would do this?'

'They might still be here…' Liz voiced all their fears.

'I still can't believe it's real. I'm going to get a closer look. Anyone coming with me?' Susanne looked at the other six women around her. It was clear that none of them wanted to go in the field.

'The gate's padlocked.' Dee nodded to a large padlock and chain.

'I can climb over. We can't call the police if it's just some art installation or practical joke.'

'Art installation! If that's art then I'm writing to the *Guardian*.'

'Do you think we should take some photos?' Trish asked, but nobody answered because they were all watching Susanne as she clambered up the metal gate with her big walking boots on, and carefully straddled the top before jumping down the other side.

Now she was actually in the field and on her own, Susanne's bravery began to dwindle. She had been so sure it couldn't be real. This wasn't the sixteenth century. They were in the twenty-first century, a modern age. But the closer she walked to it, the more her stomach clenched and knotted, pushing acidic bile up into her throat. She nearly twisted her ankle in a rut, she was so transfixed by the sight. They'd been around fifty metres from it on the lane, halfway across the open field, and now closer, the recognition that it was definitely real hit her.

Twenty metres away, she stopped and pulled her phone from her pocket to dial 999.

'There's a person!' she said to the operator, 'they've been burnt on a cross. They're dead...'

Even as she said it, she knew the body was a woman. In front of her were the charred remains of a human being, chained to a blackened wooden cross. Susanne could see where the flames had decimated her lower body but on the skull, patches of burnt flesh remained. She wanted to run. To turn away from the ghastly sight in front of her, but Susanne stood rooted to the spot in fear, unable to move. Just like the woman in front of her.

TWO

Detective Sergeant Ross Gibbons was not having a good day. The second he arrived just outside of the village of Thistleford, he knew this case was going to be trouble. For one thing, they didn't have anywhere near enough personnel to be able to create a secure cordon around the crime scene and thanks to the virality of social media, the place was already swarming with people trying to get a look at 'the witch burning'.

He had to negotiate several cars which had been abandoned along the lane, a road which was barely able to allow two-way traffic at the best of times, let alone when there were hordes of people walking around glued to their mobile phones. He used his horn and sirens more than once, getting a brief couple of seconds of pleasure in frightening the living daylights out of some of them. 'Quidnuncs', his grandmother called them. He used to find that a very old-fashioned word and invariably used far more fruity descriptors, but in polite company quidnunc would do.

The police cordon consisted of a piece of police crime scene tape stretched across the lane on both sides of the entrance to the field where their victim had been killed. Two officers were manning the tape on both sides, constantly asking people to stand back and shouting at those who were trying to scale the roadside bank to get a look. The tape ensured that nobody could see directly into the field, but Gibbons could tell that as more onlookers arrived it would take just one person to push against the flimsy tape and they'd overrun the officers.

Gibbons pulled up to the tape, hooting his horn loudly at the row of people standing along its length.

'Haven't you people got something better to do? Show some respect to the victim and get out of here,' he shouted through his window.

A couple of them looked a bit shamefaced and sloped off, but the bulk of them stayed, their morality a sneering middle finger to his authority. The buzz of getting a shot of 'the witch' to put on their social media feeds far outweighed the verbal wrath of some police officer.

'Sir, it's overwhelming,' the young police officer said as he lifted the tape to allow his car to pass underneath.

Gibbons pulled up alongside a forensics van and got on his mobile immediately.

'We need more personnel now,' he said down the phone. 'This whole area is being swamped. And get a drone team here as well; it's a big area to cover and they'll be coming in from all directions.' He knew the media would no doubt be en route by now and some of their photographers wouldn't just stand politely behind the police cordon waiting. There were probably others already trekking across the fields to come at the site from another direction, hoping to catch the police unawares.

As soon as he got out of his car and stood up, the bitter smell of burning hit him and the view of the remains of the bonfire came into view. It took him a moment to take it in. He'd been to some pretty horrific crime scenes but this was like one from a horror movie or a history book come to life. A thick wooden cross, blackened by fire, rose from the still smoking pile of wood, and tied to it was the form of a human being, also burnt but still recognisable as having once been a person. If they'd been alive at the time the fire was lit, it would have been a horrible death. How could you hate someone that much?

Two white-suited forensics officers were ahead of him in the field, bent over studying the ground. To his right, he spotted the officer who had been first on the scene, talking to a group of women that looked to be in their sixties.

'Sergeant Bashar.' Gibbons approached and extended his hand.

'DS Gibbons,' he replied, mirroring the gesture. 'These are the ladies who found the victim.'

Gibbons took the seven women in. All in good walking boots, with warm coats and a couple with small rucksacks, he didn't have to think hard to realise they were one of the many walking groups who came from town to ramble around the country.

'Can I ask how you came to find the scene?' Gibbons asked, wondering from which direction they'd come across it.

'We were walking along the road from the village, smelt the smoke and then when we got to the gate there, we could see it,' the tallest of the seven women said.

'We weren't sure if it was real at first. Thought it might be a scarecrow or an art installation,' a thin little bird of a woman added.

Gibbons nodded in empathy. It wasn't a sight anyone would expect to come across on a stroll around country lanes.

'I climbed over the gate to take a closer look,' the tall woman said again. 'Didn't want to call you unnecessarily.'

'Do forensics know?' Gibbons turned to Bashar.

'Yes, all logged. No one else has come into the field since I've been here apart from these ladies who we had to get out of the way of the crowd.'

'OK, thank you,' Gibbons said to the women now. 'Did you

see anyone else in the area, any people or cars pass you on the road?'

All seven shook their heads.

'We didn't see anyone after we'd left the village. The gate was locked when we arrived.' The tall woman nodded towards the metal gate.

'Nothing else that stood out to you?'

All seven shook their heads again.

'You're all looking a bit cold and I'm sure you're shocked and could do with getting out of here. Where do you need to get to?'

'Our cars are in the village.'

'Right, well I've been promised some more personnel, they should be here in the next ten minutes or so. Sergeant, when the transport van arrives can you get the driver to take these ladies into the village so they can get home.' He turned back to the women. 'We will probably need to contact you again for further statements, so we'll be in touch.'

Gibbons left Bashar and the walkers and headed across the field towards the bonfire and the two forensics officers. The first one in his path, a middle-aged man, looked up as he approached.

'Gibbo, you've got a right one here,' the man said, standing up and stretching his back. Oliver Weston had been working forensics longer than Ross had been on the force. He was a good bloke and a mean darts player.

'Anything you can tell me?' Ross asked him. His eyes went to the figure strapped to the wooden cross. Now he was closer it looked even more gruesome.

'We haven't touched the bonfire yet, it's still hot and smoking. Fire brigade are on their way to see what they can do without damaging any evidence. We're worried that there are pockets of heat inside the bonfire which could reignite if we start moving debris and wafting air around. I'd like to get some screens up around it, but it's quite tall so I've had to call in some specialist equipment. At least it's not looking like rain.'

'Anything on the ground? Tyre tracks?'

'We've found a boot mark in one of these furrows nearer to the gate, but I'm suspecting it might be the walker who found it. She climbed the fence and took a closer look. We're looking for evidence on the ground right now in the hope whoever did this might have dropped something, but not found anything yet.'

'How the hell can someone build a structure like this without people noticing or there being some kind of mechanical help?'

'I don't know, but what I do know is this couldn't have been done by one person in a night. I helped with our local community bonfire a couple of years ago. It was bigger than this but it took ten of us to get it built.'

A shiver ran down DS Ross Gibbons's spine.

'What could they have done to deserve this?'

Just then a yell from across the field near to the gate, distracted them. Sergeant Bashar was shouting and running towards the small copse of trees that ran down one flank of the field. Gibbons could see coloured jackets in the trees.

He swore and ran towards them, keeping one eye on the ground where fresh ruts had been scored in the earth. By the time he reached the edge of the trees, the coloured jackets had disappeared.

'Ghouls,' Bashar said to him as Gibbons reached him. 'No respect for the dead.'

'You stay here, would you, to make sure they don't come back and I'll go and sort the women out. That van should be here any minute. I'll get someone to relieve you as soon as.'

'With pleasure,' Bashar said, a look of determination on his face.

Ross knew that he'd patrol the area with the tenacity of a rottweiler.

As luck would have it, Gibbons just made it back to the women when a white transport van filled with police arrived. Sergeant Trudy Dorman jumped out first. She was a welcome sight.

'I need this whole area secured, we're getting members of the public coming from all angles trying to take photographs,' he said to her.

'No problem,' she replied and was straight onto it, organising her team efficiently and quickly.

The drone pilot was last out, hauling his black bag with him.

'We've had members of the public in that little copse of trees to the right there,' Gibbons explained to him. 'Can you do a recce for me and check there's nobody else trying to break through across our crime scene boundary?'

'Sure, I'll have her up in five minutes.'

Next, Ross spoke to the driver of the van and beckoned the seven women over to get a lift back to the village. All of them looked pale and drawn and he suspected they'd all be in need of a hot drink and a sit down.

'Can I ask you all please not to share anything about this crime scene with anyone outside of this enquiry. Something you say may compromise our investigation.'

They all nodded like school children being told off for being late to class.

Further down the lane, Ross could hear a fire engine attempting to drive through the chaos. Once the bonfire was extinguished, they'd be able to get to the victim – they couldn't waste any more time.

'Thank you for your help today,' he said to the ladies, attempting a smile, before saying his goodbyes and turning away from the group.

'Sir, have you seen this?'

Ross looked round to see the drone pilot studying his screen with a frown.

He peered over the man's shoulder at the small image. 'What the—!' he exclaimed. As though what they'd already seen couldn't get any weirder...

There, clear as day on the drone's image, a pattern was scored into the earth around the bonfire. A circle surrounding a flower petal pattern that radiated out from the bonfire.

'What does it mean?' the drone operator asked him.

All thoughts of errant members of the public disappeared from Gibbons's mind.

'I don't know, but we're going to need some expert help with this one.'

THREE

Harrison stood back and surveyed the fruits of three very frustrating hours of labour. He'd ordered the flat-pack wardrobe because with Tanya, his girlfriend, staying over so often, she needed more than just the tiny space available in his own wardrobe. Besides, he'd told himself, he needed one in the spare bedroom anyway. It wasn't as if she was moving in or anything.

He'd taken a day off work. As well as the wardrobe, he'd had the plumber coming round to sort an issue with the tap in the kitchen, plus there was a new double air fryer being delivered. Tanya said she liked cooking with her air fryer and as Harrison wanted to kick the need for ultra-processed TV dinners, he was all for more home cooking. This was all a long way from his single bachelor days when his London Docklands apartment was silent except for when he worked out or listened to his Native American meditation music. If you'd asked him a year ago, he'd have been aghast at the thought of waking up most mornings with someone by his side, but the truth was, he'd grown to quite enjoy it.

He had expected to take just an hour to make the wardrobe. He was handy with tools and his body strength meant he should make short work of the lifting and shifting that was needed. What he hadn't allowed for were the various hurdles along the way, which irritated him due to the inefficient use of his time. First, the instructions. It took him around twenty minutes just to work out what they were trying to say. Had they been Ancient Egyptian hieroglyphics he'd have had an easier job of it. As it was, he felt like he was trying to make sense of a piece of abstract art. Once he'd finally mastered them, he was about halfway through when he found a piece that he hadn't used and seemed to have no purpose at all. That sent his alarm bells ringing. Had he missed a step? Was this a vital piece of the wardrobe? This wasted fifteen minutes of his life that he would never get back, while he worked out that it was actually a surplus part used in the packing and he could ignore it.

Once the wardrobe was finally finished and he'd checked that it was fully functional, he stepped back and surveyed his work with the feeling he'd just triumphed in some epic challenge. The man who was six feet two, very fit, intelligent, and dedicated to getting the bad guys and saving victims, didn't miss the irony. He was just glad his friend DI Jack Salter hadn't been round to witness the spectacle.

The plumber had been and gone in an hour and Harrison just had the arrival of the air fryer to wait for. Once he'd ensured the wardrobe was in place, he'd got his running gear on, ready to head out as soon as the delivery guy came. While he waited, he made himself a herbal tea and sat on the sofa in front of the big window which overlooked the Thames. He watched the progress of several small boats meandering along its surface, like woodlice on a woodland path. The water sparkled today, reflecting the clear sky and sunshine which had miraculously appeared after days of grey and rain. Green borders were springing up again along the brown riverbanks and there was a new energy in the air, charged with the promise of summer.

Harrison was distracted from the view by the sound of his

mobile phone ringing. He'd left it in the bedroom where he'd been building the wardrobe and so he went in search of it, expecting it to either be the delivery driver, or Tanya checking up on how his day at home had gone. She knew full well that perpetual workaholic was more in his make-up than stay-at-home DIYer.

But the caller wasn't Tanya; it was Ryan, his assistant, which could only mean that something important had cropped up with work.

'Yo, boss,' Ryan's voice filled his ear. 'How's it going with the wardrobe? Has it beaten you yet?'

'Nope. All good. It's done.'

'Really? That's impressive. Takes me three times longer than I expect it to take and something always ends up wonky.'

Harrison looked at the newly built wardrobe in front of him with a critical eye. 'No. I think we're good, but I have to admit it took a little longer than I'd expected it to.'

'Ah, the joys of flat packs.' Ryan smirked down the phone. 'Well, glad you've conquered it because we've got a job in. They want you to go to a sleepy little village called Thistleford where apparently nothing happens, until now. Someone has burnt a witch on a wooden cross.'

As this piece of information hit him, Harrison's doorbell sounded. He walked back out the spare room towards his front door.

'Witch?' he clarified.

'Yeah, you know like in the Middle Ages when they thought any old woman who lived alone with a cat was a witch.'

'OK, hang on...' Harrison opened his front door expecting to see a delivery person outside. There was nobody. He looked down. A big brown box was on the floor. He picked it up and brought it into the flat. 'Right, go on.'

'Local police are in panic mode,' Ryan continued. 'She was only discovered this morning and already they've been swamped by the media and all the usual social media vloggers, and apparently they're besieged by violence against women protestors and a whole load of modern-day witches and religious fanatics.'

'Do they know who the victim is?' Harrison put the box on the side in the kitchen and took out some scissors.

'Not yet. Seb at the NCA wants us on it ASAP. He's worried it has the potential to escalate.'

'He's probably right,' Harrison replied, cutting the tape on the box and thinking about the man he reported to at the National Crime Agency, Detective Inspector Sebastian Bartholomew. He pulled the flaps back on the box and saw the packaging for his air fryer. Parcel identified, Harrison returned to his cup of tea by the sofa and looked out the window once more at the Thames, flowing past oblivious. Life didn't stand still and neither could he. 'How far is it?' he asked Ryan.

'One hundred and eleven point six miles,' Ryan replied.

Harrison smiled. Ryan was always on the ball and knew exactly what he needed.

'OK, tell him I'll head down there right away. Send me the details would you.'

'They're already on their way to you.'

'Cheers, Ryan, I'll let you know what else I need once I've got there.'

'No problemo, I'll hold the fort while you're gone.'

Ryan and Harrison were the only two staff in the Ritualistic Behavioural Crime unit, which had originally been within the London Metropolitan police, but was now part of the National Crime Agency due to the need across the country for Dr Harrison Lane's expertise. As Harrison spent most of his time at various crime scenes around the country, Ryan was usually the one left fielding the requests for help. He'd become quite adept at deciphering some of the symbols and imagery they were sent, having developed an intelligent software programme with the information Harrison gave him. Of course, he wasn't a behavioural psychologist like his boss, and so when it came to anything other than being able to tell what a symbol was, he had to refer it up. What he was good at, was research and finding information on the internet. If it was out there, Ryan would find it.

While Harrison turned on his Harley-Davidson Road King bike, feeling the deep rumble of its engine reverberating through his body, Ryan settled himself into his desk chair with a large bag of cheese Wotsits and set about researching the area of Thistleford and its history.

FOUR

Had he not already had a day of incongruous and strange sights, DS Ross Gibbons might have been more taken aback by the man striding towards him across the field. Dressed in black leathers, with a physique more suited to an action hero than an expert in ritualistic crimes, Dr Harrison Lane was not the kind of man he'd been expecting to see – but then Ross guessed that Dr Lane probably got that reaction a lot. Whatever the ritualistic behavioural crime psychologist looked like, he was glad to see him.

'Dr Lane, thank you for coming,' Ross held his hand out and had it enveloped by a strong grip. 'We've had to put up a tall screen around the victim,' Ross said, nodding towards the canvas screens which flapped very gently in the slight breeze. 'Not an easy crime scene to protect,' he added unnecessarily. 'We were hoping you could throw some light on what all this is about. There's not too much to tell you at all.'

'That's fine. I'd rather make my own observations initially,' Dr Lane finally spoke, interrupting Gibbons as though he didn't want the DS to say another word.

'Of course, no problem.'

'Can I go inside the screens and take a look?'

'Yes absolutely, forensics are in there with a fire officer. They're assessing the best way to access the victim.'

'Would it be possible to be in there alone? It helps my concentration.'

'Right, well,' Ross said, a little taken aback. 'Of course, but if you don't mind, I'll have to observe just for the crime scene record, but I won't disturb you.'

Dr Lane nodded in agreement, but said nothing more as they walked across to the entrance. He waited while Ross asked the others to leave and seemed to be meditating or sleeping on his feet. He stood, eyes closed, breathing deeply. Ross waited, wondering if he should tell him that they were ready and he could go in, but didn't think he should interrupt him. A tickle came to Ross's throat and he swallowed several times to try not to cough. Then, Dr Lane's eyes snapped open and without a word, he walked into the enclosure where the bonfire and their unfortunate victim were waiting.

Ross waited at the entrance, well out of the way, and watched the ritualistic crime expert at work. He seemed to stand there for ages at first, just looking, studying every minute detail of the scene in front of him. Then, he slowly walked around the structure, looking at the ground and at the debris of the fire as well as the victim from all angles.

There was no emotion on his face, it remained rigid in its concentration, no signs of recognition or understanding, no indications that the horror in front of him was making any impact.

Finally, once Dr Lane had walked a full circle a couple of times around the bonfire, he approached Ross.

'Thanks,' he said and disappeared through the entrance of the enclosed crime scene and into the field.

Ross followed him out, slightly bemused. He'd been expecting to have a conversation or to get some kind of reaction, but instead, he'd been left to stand and watch as Harrison Lane went striding off around the field. Not entirely sure what was happening now, he gave the forensic team and fire officers the go ahead to head back inside and waited for Dr Lane to finish his walk around. A lot of his focus initially was on the ground, and he stopped and peered at a few spots before continuing his walk.

Finally, he came striding back to Ross.

'Still no idea of who the victim is yet?' Harrison asked him.

Ross shook his head. 'No. We are thinking that it's a woman though. We're hoping to get her down in the next couple of hours. There's something else you should see too.' Ross took out his phone. 'We had a drone go up and this is what it saw.' He held his phone out for Dr Lane to view the screen. On it was the image of the circle and the criss-crossing flower petals radiating out from the bonfire.

Dr Harrison Lane slowly nodded.

'Yes, I can see that on the ground. It's an apotropaic mark, sometimes called a witch's mark. You can find them in churches and old buildings. They were said to protect you from evil and malevolent witchcraft.'

'So you think that whoever did this was trying to stop the victim's power from escaping the fire? That they really believed she was a witch?'

'I'd say that's a possibility. Fire is also used for cleansing. If they believed she'd been touched by evil, the fire could have been a cleanser and the symbol was to protect her. I know the end result is the same for the victim, but they are slightly different motivations. Bizarrely one is done out of concern for her well-being, the other is because they feared her and thought her intrinsically evil. However, there's something else that to me indicates they did believe her evil, or at least deserving of punishment.'

Ross looked at him expectantly, but Harrison just beckoned him to follow and walked off, scanning the ground.

'Here,' he said, stopping and crouching down next to a rock the size of a large potato.

'A stone?' Ross replied, his brow deeply furrowed with confusion. 'There are always stones in fields. Look here's another,' he said, pointing to one poking from the ground where they'd just walked.

'Is there anything you notice about this particular stone?'

'It's clean.'

Harrison nodded.

'Leviticus, the law of holiness, "A man or woman who calls up ghosts or spirits shall be put to death. The people shall stone them; their blood shall be on their own heads."'

'You mean you think they stoned the victim first? Is that in the Bible?' Ross stared at the rock lying on the ground beside them.

'Yes, Old Testament, God speaking to Moses about those who practised any form of witchcraft or spiritualism. If you look around the fire, there are several of these clean rocks lying on the surface, all the others are muddy or half buried, and these are a slightly different colour too. I think these stones were brought to the field for a purpose which was to stone the victim before the bonfire was lit.'

'So what you're saying is that whoever did this really believed in witchcraft and magic? That they are some kind of religious fanatics?'

'What we are seeing certainly suggests that.'

There was silence between the two men for a few moments as Ross's head was filled with the violent images of a group of people stoning and then setting light to the victim.

'What do you think about the scene as a whole? Anything that stands out to you?'

Dr Lane looked at him then. 'What, you mean apart from the fact it's a witch burning from the Middle Ages and this is 2024?'

DS Gibbons shuffled on his feet. 'Yes. I mean we've got no witnesses, nobody noticed this bloody great big bonfire being built.'

'What are you getting at DS Gibbons?'

'I'm trying to work out how the hell it got here without anyone local noticing it.'

'Not by the hand of one man, that's for sure.'

'That's what I'm thinking.' Ross looked glum.

'This was a group of people. The ground around the bonfire is well trodden and while I know your team have been in there, it's not just from their feet. I can see areas of the ground which are compacted and have ash on top which hasn't been disturbed. It's impossible to say how many people were here, but you're right, it would have taken a fair number to get the wood stacked. Then, how was the wooden cross put into the ground? It looks strong. Was there really nothing in this field before this morning? They must have put the cross up, tied the victim to it, and then had to build the fire around them. You're looking at a few hours of work.'

'What are you saying, Dr Lane? Are you insinuating there's some kind of magic gone on here? It's given me the creeps this has. What did she do to deserve this mob punishment?'

'I see this reaction quite often in the kind of cases that I look into, DS Gibbons. If this poor victim was burnt alive then it is a horrifying crime, but what we have to keep in mind is that it is just that, a crime the same as any other you investigate. There's nothing magical or satanic, nothing that can't be explained. Your brain is remembering the stories and myths that our society has ingrained in your psyche from the fairy tales you'd have read as a child, to the horror movies you've seen as an adult.'

'That still doesn't explain how this all came to be here. I didn't see any obvious tractor treads by the gate; they're big heavy vehicles.' He frowned at Dr Lane and looked around.

'No, and it's the only obvious route in. The ground is harder up the top of the field but I don't think they used a tractor; it was something lighter. Maybe an articulated boom for example. There are some marks on the ground to the right of the bonfire, square indents into the earth. Perhaps where the vehicle's stabilisers were deployed when they lifted the cross up.'

'I didn't see the holes,' Ross said incredulously.

'You were focusing on the bonfire and the horror of that scene. But the evidence to explain its existence is around it.'

'What about the furrows used to create the witch's mark?'

'Possibly a hand-operated tool or mechanised machine. The furrows aren't deep. I'm no expert in gardening and farming, but perhaps one of those single-person rotovators or something similar you'd use on a smallholding? This was well-planned and depending on how many people were involved, would still have taken hours to execute. If I'm right about the kinds of machinery, you can get some which aren't very loud, but at night they would have been easier to hear.'

'There's nothing between here and Thistleford, which is the nearest village, so that's where we need to start. Someone must have heard or seen something. I'll be glad to get away from here. And you're right, Dr Lane. This is murder, not some kind of spiritual event – and I'm going to make sure whoever committed this crime finds themselves in a very real prison for a long time.'

FIVE

DS Ross Gibbons was just briefing the forensics officers about the stones and their potential for DNA and blood traces, when their attention was grabbed by something happening at the gate entrance.

'I demand to know what is going on,' the raised voice of a well-spoken man cut through the rest of the hubbub.

'Sir,' the officer dealing with him called to Ross. 'This gentleman says that this is his field.'

'Right, let him through a moment, would you?' DS Gibbons motioned.

Harrison looked at the tall man who claimed to be the field owner. He was well dressed in a country style: a waxed Barbour jacket and brown corduroy trousers with a smart looking shirt. His shoes were Oxford brogues.

'This is my field, what's going on here? Are they holding some kind of festival?'

'Mr—?' DS Gibbons asked.

'Nick Rogers. If that lot have organised something illegal on my land, it's not my fault. I've rented it to them but I can't be held responsible for what they do, you know. They'll be hearing from my lawyers though.' He tried to peer around Harrison and DS Gibbons into the field.

'What lot are you referring to, Mr Rogers?' Gibbons asked.

'The lot up at Harmony House. A bunch of reprobates, some kind of back-to-the-dark-ages cult, but they pay more than the local farmers can in rent.'

'Dark ages cult?'

'Yes, don't know much about them really. Nobody does. Keep themselves to themselves. All I know is they haven't done a thing with this field since they started renting it, apart from ploughing it now and then to keep the weeds down. Use horses and old ploughs to do that, would you believe? Said they are letting the toxic chemicals wash from the earth so they can grow organic. But they're odd, secretive people.'

'What's Harmony House?'

'It's the big manor just up the road there. You can't get through the gates now, they keep them locked.'

'Right, well thank you for the information, Mr Rogers, but this is unfortunately a crime scene and so we are going to have to ask you to leave for now. Can you give me your contact details and address and I'll arrange to come and talk to you.'

'Crime scene? What's been going on then? You know I've heard rumours that the Harmony House lot are all ex-convicts... If they've started killing each other then it wouldn't surprise me!' He stopped and looked at DS Gibbons, clearly hoping to be given some information back. When none was forthcoming, he continued. 'I'm at Thistleford House, the biggest house in the village, everyone knows where to find me.' With that, Nick Rogers marched off, ducking underneath the police tape.

'Well, that was interesting,' DS Gibbons said to Harrison as they watched the back of Nick Rogers disappear into the crowd of onlookers. 'A cult that lives like they're in the dark ages.

Perhaps they believe in witchcraft and stoning and burning people to death too.'

Harrison was just formulating a considered response that coached against jumping to conclusions due to the misconceptions around witch trials, when they were interrupted again.

'Sir,' a police constable walked up to Harrison and DS Gibbons. 'Looks like we may have a possible ID for the victim. We've just had a call from the village, a Charley Jones has gone round to her employer's cottage, a Ms Louise Swift, and found the place ransacked. There's no sign of Ms Swift and she's not answering her mobile, plus there's a load of religious-looking graffiti been daubed inside.'

'Thank you, constable, is there anything to suggest Ms Swift had any kind of witchcraft interest?'

'I'm not sure, sir, but apparently she's a medium, you know one of those clairvoyant people who do fortune telling and talked to the dead.'

'Right, address?'

'Two, the High Street, Thistleford.'

Harrison followed DS Gibbons's car along the narrow country lanes and down into the village of Thistleford which ran along the middle of a shallow valley, flanked by fields and woodland. A single road snaked through the tiny village, little more than just a hamlet. Harrison estimated there were about twenty houses, and a tiny pub and shop in the centre. Most of the buildings were built from the same grey stone with wooden sash windows painted white and slate-tiled roofs. It was a picture-perfect English scene, the kind of place Americans would love. As they entered the village, he noted the large stone house, set slightly back from the rest, with a manicured front garden and its own gravelled entrance. That must be where Nick Rogers lived. A police squad car was parked up just a couple of cottages along from the big house.

'We need to put on protective clothing,' DS Gibbons said as he walked up to join Harrison, who had parked his bike. 'I don't want to contaminate the cottage with anything from the field.' He handed Harrison a white suit, gloves, and overshoes. 'Sorry about the fit, just got my size in the boot.'

Harrison looked at the detective in front of him. He was average or below average in height and slender build. Harrison was a big build at six feet two. This was going to be a challenge, he'd need to reduce his layers of clothing.

'Can I leave my jacket and jumper in your car?' Harrison asked.

'Of course, whatever you need,' Ross replied.

Clothing layers duly deposited, Harrison carefully pulled on the suit over his T-shirt and black jeans. It was an extremely tight fit. He'd have usually worn at least one, probably two sizes larger, but thanks to the fact they were made to fit over outer clothes, he was able to just squeeze into it without breaking the zip – just. Although yoga bends were going to be out of the question.

'So, what we got?' Gibbons asked the police constable who was stood in the doorway.

'Sir. A Charley Jones, who lives in the village, arrived at the property forty-five minutes ago. She works part time for Ms Louise Swift. She's her digital assistant apparently. Anyway, she knocked and got no reply, so used the key that Ms Swift had given her. When she entered she found that the house had been turned upside down and there was no sign of Ms Swift.'

'Anyone else been in?'

'Just me, sir. I wanted to ensure that there was nobody inside needing assistance.'

'Where's Miss Jones now?'

'Gone back to her house, sir. She lives at Foxley Cottage, next door to the pub, with her parents.'

'And why are we thinking that the homeowner might be our victim, could she not have just gone away for the weekend and been burgled?'

'Miss Jones said that she had asked her to come into work today as she was running a whole series of medium readings. Does them online apparently. She said she wouldn't have chosen to miss those as she's been building up her following.'

'Following?'

'On TikTok, sir.'

Gibbons groaned, which Harrison took to mean he was neither a fan, nor a regular TikToker.

'Presume she's tried contacting her?'

'She has rung her mobile, sir, and no reply.'

Harrison could see nothing on the outside of the house which would indicate anything out of the ordinary inside. The curtains were still drawn in the windows, but there wasn't anything else that suggested its occupant had been practising Wicca or that a crime had taken place. He followed DS Gibbons in through the small doorway.

The first thing he noticed was that it was an unremarkable hallway, apart from the black witch's mark that had been roughly spray-painted onto the wall opposite a large oak-framed mirror.

'I take it that's the witch's sign again?' Gibbons said to Harrison.

'It is.'

Harrison followed the DS into a small sitting area on the right-hand side where they saw another witch's mark on the wall and also a crucifix sprayed beside it. Underneath were the words, *'Do not turn to mediums or seek out spiritualists, for you will be defiled by them. I am the Lord your God.'*

'Bible?' Gibbons questioned, nodding at the wall.

'Yes. Leviticus again.'

Both men fell silent as they surveyed the room. It was filled with traditional oak furniture that went with the age of the property. But this room had once had a certain ambience to it. There were candles everywhere, shelves of books with various crystals, a smashed fortune-telling globe. Most of the books had been pulled from the shelves and pages ripped from them. These were the ones about spiritualism and spell books, psychic skill guidebooks and the like. The decor wasn't Gypsy Rose, it was a little more tasteful than that, but there was no doubting that in here she would have told fortunes and consulted the spirits for clients.

'No TV,' was DS Gibbons's observation.

'Wouldn't go with the image,' Harrison replied. 'She obviously saw clients in here.'

'Someone clearly didn't agree with what she did,' Gibbons added, walking out of the room and back into the hallway. He went straight ahead this time, toward the kitchen.

Immediately, Harrison's eyes were drawn to the jars of herbs lining the shelf. There was a pestle and mortar in the middle of the kitchen table and a supermarket carrier bag on a chair. He peered into the bag and examined the contents of the mortar where he could see the residue of ground herbs and what appeared to be white powder along with the crushed greenery. Gibbons had carried on through a door on the other side of the kitchen.

Harrison scanned the kitchen which also had a small sitting area with a comfy sofa and TV, clearly where she relaxed.

'Well they did this place over good and proper,' Gibbons said from the other room.

Harrison followed him to the doorway of a small office which was bedecked in fortune-telling and Wicca decor, much of which was now lying in a jumble around the room. A computer screen with a webcam on top had been smashed and there were tarot cards ripped up and scattered like snowflakes on top of the mess.

'Well, on the evidence, I'd say we could well have found the identity of our victim, or at the very least, somebody who was involved in what went on last night. Although it's possible Ms Swift managed to keep away and it's not her in that field, so we need to keep an open mind. Let's have a quick look upstairs and then get forensics in here. I want to have a chat with Miss Jones and then head to the station to get this inquiry fully underway.'

'I'll just wander around for a bit longer if that's OK?' Harrison said to him.

'Go ahead, you know the drill with forensics but if there's anything that stands out to you let me know. I wouldn't have a clue what any of this spiritual stuff is.'

As Gibbons walked off, Harrison heard him talking on his mobile phone and asking the forensics team to come to the cottage. Their first priority was going to be confirming if the body on the bonfire was Louise Swift or not. Louise could be somewhere fearing for her life. Harrison's priority was getting to know her, finding out as much as he could about her life and what she did. Dead or alive, somewhere along the way she'd upset people. The question was who – and what exactly had she done?

SIX

Charley Jones was a young woman with long brown hair, and a thin face that told of too many days inside on computers and not enough time outside in the fresh air. Her mother had answered the door to DS Gibbons and Harrison, folding her arms over her chest, and planting her feet firmly in the doorway.

'She's had a terrible shock, you know, and she's quite fragile. I don't want you upsetting her.'

'I promise that we will be as gentle as possible, Mrs Jones, we just want to ask her some questions about Louise Swift and her work.'

Mrs Jones shook her head and pulled her mouth down. 'I can't believe what's gone on. Do you know where she is? What's happened to her? I hear there's been some incident up in the fields.'

'We can't confirm anything at this stage, Mrs Jones. We are in the early stages of our enquiries.'

'We're a close-knit community here, you know. Everyone knows her. It's upsetting for us all.'

'Yes we appreciate that and we will do all we can to support you, but our first priority is to get to the bottom of where Miss Swift might be.'

Mrs Jones let out a big sigh, gave them both one more look over and then stepped out of the way of the doorway and let the two men enter her cottage.

'Charley! Charley! The police are here and want to talk to you,' Mrs Jones shouted up the stairs. Then she turned to them. 'Spends all her time up there on that computer, you know. Never comes down to watch the TV with us. We only see her when she wants feeding.'

'It's the same in my house,' DS Gibbons said, smiling.

Harrison looked at him surprised, he didn't seem old enough to have a teenage child and he wondered if he'd just said that to create empathy, or was telling the truth.

'You can go on in,' Mrs Jones said to them both, nodding them into a sitting room. 'Need a tea or coffee?'

'Oh, I'd love a good brew, yes please,' Gibbons replied, his face lighting up. Harrison knew he'd been up in the field for hours and it wasn't that warm a day, despite the spring sun.

'Just a glass of water if you please,' Harrison said to her expectant face.

'Milk and sugar?' she asked Gibbons as she turned to leave them.

'Just a little milk, thanks,' he replied, a satisfied smile already on his face at the prospect of drinking his tea.

Harrison heard the sound of soft footsteps coming down the stairs and then some hushed whispering outside in the hallway. Charley joined them, silently slipping into the room and sitting down, barely even making eye contact.

'Charley, I'm Detective Sergeant Ross Gibbons, and this is my colleague Dr Harrison Lane. Thank you for notifying us about Louise Swift's cottage.'

She gave a small shrug, still staring down at her feet. 'Has something happened to her? I've seen the photos on social media. Is it her?'

'Sorry?'

'Up there in the field. She wouldn't have missed those sessions. It has to be her. Someone trashed her office.' Charley looked up briefly at them before dropping her eyes down again.

'We are investigating the incident in the field. What have you seen?'

'It's on TikTok, just search hashtag witch and you'll see them.'

'OK, but right now nothing has been confirmed and we've got no evidence linking Ms Swift, so can you give us any information about your employer?'

She gave another shrug. 'What do you wanna know?'

'Did she have any family? Any friends she might have gone to stay with?'

Charley shook her head. 'Don't think so. She moved here two years ago and everyone liked her. Never once heard her talk about family or other friends and no one has ever visited. She told me it's just her. I got the impression she'd come here to leave something behind, you know what I mean?' Charley paused.

Harrison thought that was quite insightful for a young woman and wondered if it was an original idea or one that other villagers held.

'When she arrived she helped lots of us,' Charley continued. 'Helped me with my anxiety. She was amazing.'

'Do you know anyone who didn't appreciate her? Was she worried about anything or anyone? Was she receiving any threats from a religious group for example?'

'No.' Charley looked away.

Harrison noticed a slight change in her body language and guessed that Gibbons had as well because he didn't immediately ask another question, but gave her a moment to consider what he'd already asked her. When she said nothing more he continued.

'She hadn't changed in her behaviour or how she seemed to you at all?'

Charley shook her head.

'How long have you been working for her?'

'About two months. It was only a couple of days a week and when she needed extra help. Today she had a whole load of client sessions booked in. I was gonna help her run them all.'

'Client sessions? So she was expecting visitors?'

'No. Online. She does do in-person readings, but mostly for local people.'

'Do you have access to her computer?'

'Yeah. She had a laptop. Sometimes I helped her film too. I guess I should put a message up on her TikTok and YouTube channels.'

'No, not just yet please, we haven't any information as to what may have happened to Ms Swift and certainly no proof that she is the murder victim.'

'Murder victim!'

'Yes, the person who has been killed in the field,' DS Gibbons replied.

'Yeah, OK, I guess I hadn't really thought of it as like actual murder.'

'What would you have thought it was then?'

'I dunno, I guess revenge or some kind of punishment killing.'

'That's still murder, Ms Jones.'

Charley looked out the window as though she was searching for some kind of guidance from outside.

'Is there any reason why you think Louise should have been punished?' Harrison spoke now, watching her body language and mannerisms closely.

She seemed to snap back into the room. 'No. No of course not.'

But Harrison was sure he saw an imperceptible nod of her head. At that moment, the shadow that had been in the doorway came into view.

'How are we getting on? Here's your tea, detective,' Mrs Jones said in an overly cheerful tone. 'And your water,' she continued, handing a glass to Harrison. 'How are you holding up, Charley?' she addressed her daughter directly.

'Yeah, OK I think,' she said to her mother.

A glance exchanged between them.

'Can I ask, does the village have much to do with what goes on at Harmony House?' DS Gibbons asked after taking a large gulp of his tea.

'No. We occasionally see them wandering around the fields, or lanes. My Kevin, that's Charley's dad, saw them collecting wood a couple of weeks back. They don't seem to want anything to do with us and quite frankly that's how we'd like to keep it. They're a bunch of ruffians. God knows what they get up to at that place, a load of men on their own.'

'Did Louise Swift have anything to do with them?' DS Gibbons asked Charley.

She threw a quick glance at her mother. 'I'm not sure, maybe.'

'Maybe? What makes you think she might have?'

'Well, I think she knew one of them.'

'One of the Harmony House residents?'

'Yeah. She didn't tell me much but I saw her talking to one of them in the lanes. I think they were arguing.'

'Could you describe what this man looked like?'

'Mmmh, it was a couple of weeks ago, but he was kind of skinny, with long grey hair.'

'Any idea of his age?'

'A bit older than Mum and Dad's age, I'd say.'

'We're both nearly fifty,' her mother interjected.

'Tall or short?'

'He was quite a bit taller than she was and he had a moustache and long beard.'

'Like a Father Christmas beard and moustache?'

'No, it was dark grey, not white, and kind of a skinnier beard.'

'OK, thank you.'

'Do you know if she did any readings for them at Harmony House?'

'Maybe. I only work two days a week with her. She has a diary.' Charley suddenly brightened, looking at DS Gibbons. 'Didn't like doing her diary online so she had a black desk diary and wrote everything down. Said it helped her to connect with her clients better when she wrote their names and saw them on paper.'

'OK, thank you. We can look for that. We're going to need to talk to you again, but I think that's all for today. Once we've located Louise's laptop we'll need the password from you.'

'That's easy, it's crystal ball and a pound sign. All lowercase.'

'Thanks.' DS Gibbons made a note and then downed the last of his tea.

Harrison finished his water as they stood up to leave.

'Does the pub here do rooms?' Harrison asked Mrs Jones.

'Next door? No. It's literally just a one room bar in there. We run it as a bit of a co-operative really. It's our village meeting place; we don't often get outsiders coming in, although visitors are welcome if they do.'

'Did Louise go to the pub?'

'Oh yes. She even held some reading sessions there.'

'Right, thanks,' Harrison said, standing and then following DS Gibbons out.

'I hope you find out where she is,' Charley's mother said to them as they left.

'We will.' DS Gibbons smiled reassuringly at her.

As soon as they were out of earshot, Gibbons turned to Harrison.

'So, what did you make of that then?'

'I'd say Charley is holding back. She definitely knows more than she's letting on and is clearly convinced Louise is dead because she kept referring to her in the past tense.'

'Yup, exactly my feeling too. Question is, why and what is it she knows? Are they involved or are they scared? Right now, I've got no idea which, but this afternoon we need to go and pay a visit to Harmony House because that place keeps cropping up.'

SEVEN

Harrison followed DS Gibbons to the incident room which had been set up in the police station in the nearest town, about ten miles away. Right now it was just an empty room with a few desks in it, but some additional computers and other equipment were being brought over from the regional office.

'I need feeding,' Ross Gibbons announced to Harrison the second they arrived and had parked up. 'There's a good little bakery next door, you coming?'

Harrison hadn't felt hungry until he'd mentioned it, but now the bubbles of hunger rumbled around his stomach. 'Sure,' he said.

'I appreciate you coming to help out,' Ross said to him as they walked to the shop. 'I get what you said about this basically being a murder, same as any other we cover, but it's receiving a ton of media attention and I need to be able to cut all the witchcraft claptrap out of the equation and just look at the bare facts. I'm hoping you can help me do that.'

'Of course. But what you have to bear in mind is that the witchcraft claptrap as you call it, can instil some very strong beliefs in people, like any religion. It can be behind all sorts of motivations, fear usually, sometimes other emotions. We need to fully understand what Louise Swift was doing in order to be able to work out the motivations of her killers, assuming she is our victim.'

'Yes and what the hell that lot at Harmony House are up to. If it's some kind of fundamental religious cult up there then we could have a cut and dried motive. Christianity and the like don't take too kindly to those who dabble in the dark arts, do they?'

'It depends on what kind of fundamental religious beliefs they have, but possibly,' Harrison said. A little alarm bell was going off in his head. He wondered if the Harmony House group would turn out to be easy scapegoats.

'I also want to know what she was doing before she arrived at Thistleford. In my experience, the past can often raise an ugly head and bite people. Talking of which, here we are.'

They'd arrived in the bakery where Harrison was immediately captured by a tray of freshly cooked Cornish pasties. The slight bubble of hunger in his stomach instantly turned to a serious growl as his eyes fell on the golden pastry parcels lined up in front of him. He ordered two.

'They're probably not going to want us going up to Harmony House if it's a closed cult,' Harrison said to the detective as they left the shop.

'No. Let's do some more digging first. They'll claim religious persecution if we get too heavy handed, but as they are the tenants of the field in which our victim met their death, I think we have an absolute right to go and ask a few questions.'

Harrison wondered if DS Gibbons had ever tried to get information from a cult before. It wasn't as easy as most people presumed it would be in the modern world.

. . .

By the time they got back to the office, several other officers had started to congregate ready for the initial briefing. While they waited for someone from forensics to join them, Harrison and Ross Gibbons ate the contents of their greasy paper bags. Meanwhile, Harrison texted Ryan.

> Can you see what you can find out about Louise Swift, she's a medium and has YouTube and TikTok channels. Also a place called Harmony House which is just outside of Thistleford village. There's some kind of commune living there, possibly a cult.

Seconds later he got a text back.

> On it.

A man that Harrison had seen in the field earlier wearing a forensic oversuit walked into the room and DS Gibbons stood up and went to the front.

'OK, we're all here now, so let's just put our heads together and see what we've covered and what we still need to do,' Gibbons said to the room. 'We don't have all our equipment yet, but I'm going to use these whiteboards for now to get some thoughts down.' Gibbons turned and wrote Louise's name on the board.

'OK. We don't yet know the identity of our victim, but we have a missing person, Louise Swift, whose property has been vandalised by somebody who seems to think she is or was evil. We can't trace Ms Swift, she's not answering her phone and she didn't turn up for her work commitments, which means she's likely either on the run because she's involved somehow, or she is our victim in the field. I need somebody working on her background. She was a self-proclaimed medium, arrived in Thistleford about two years ago.

'Where was she before? What had she been doing? Who

were her associates? What was the nature of her work, could she have made enemies? But we do need to keep an open mind at this stage until the victim's identity is confirmed so don't assume it is her, or that she's involved. We're not even a hundred per cent sure the victim is female, so ears to the ground. Listen to everything people are telling you. I don't want us to miss anything because we're being blinkered to just one possibility.' He looked around the room making sure everyone had understood.

'What we do know is that the field in which the victim was burnt, is owned by a Nick Rogers who seems to think himself the squire of the village, but he's rented it to a group who live at Harmony House, which I'm told is some kind of commune. Is it a cult? Are they religious fanatics who might have taken umbrage at what they could have seen as evil magic powers? Did our victim have any links to them?'

'Sir,' a detective raised his hand. 'Do we assume that it's about witchcraft?'

'Right, time to introduce you all to Dr Harrison Lane from the Ritualistic Behavioural Crime unit. Dr Lane here is an expert in all things religious and ritualistic and is going to advise us in this investigation. Dr Lane, do you have anything that could help us at this stage?'

Harrison stood up to greet the eyes which had all swivelled round in his direction. 'It's early days yet and I need to do a lot more groundwork but, it looks as though the murder style was akin to that commonly believed to have been used against witches in the Middle Ages. But, there is one thing which makes me hesitant and that was that this wasn't the typical type of punishment for this area. In England and indeed America, witches were mostly executed by hanging, not by burning, although that seems to have become the modern-day interpretation. Burnings were more prevalent in Scotland. However, I also believe that the victim was stoned before being set alight.

This is a punishment written in the Old Testament for witch-craft and mediums, and therefore more indicative of a killer or killers who were using religious beliefs to justify their actions.'

Harrison paused, ensuring he had everyone with him. The room of faces was focused intently on what he was saying.

He continued. 'Furrowed into the soil around the bonfire, was an apotropaic mark, or witch's mark. We see these on old buildings, sometimes in churches. They can take different forms, but this one I've seen before. A circle, or several circles, within which appears to be petal-like shapes branching out from the centre. You'll often find it in various forms and called a Witch's knot in modern Wicca. It was supposed to ward off bad witches and evil, a protective symbol. The fact the bonfire is at the centre of this mark seems to imply that whoever drew it was likely trying to contain the victim's power, although they could possibly have been protecting her.'

'Protecting her? They killed her,' the same detective said to Harrison incredulously.

'Yes, to us that is obvious. But it's possible they felt they were helping her, cleansing her soul. I'm not saying that was the motivation, but as there are two potentials, we have to consider both at this stage.'

'But both assume that they believe that witches are real today. How can anyone believe that in our modern world?'

'Well, without wishing to offend anyone, you could also ask how in today's scientifically advanced world, anyone could believe that Adam and Eve were the first humans, that Moses parted the Red Sea, Noah built his ark to save the world, or even that Jesus was resurrected. The facts presented to people are not necessarily interpreted the same by all of us. It's the same reason that conspiracy theorists are absolutely adamant about their view of something, whether it's that a vaccine doesn't work for example, despite the huge weight of scientific, medical and practical evidence that says it does. It's called motivated reasoning. If we start with a basic belief of something then we look for further evidence, no matter how flimsy, to support that belief and we discount the other facts as lies by some malicious entity; whether it's the government, the devil, or some other cabal, working to destroy the truth. If you have a belief in God and the devil, then it's not a major next step to begin to believe that there are those who do the devil's work; and you'll find plenty of people throughout history who have sworn this to be true.'

The detective frowned and nodded thoughtfully.

'I forgot to mention that Dr Lane is a psychologist as well as a ritualistic crime expert,' DS Gibbons said, raising his eyebrows genially. 'And, somewhat of a tracking expert too I understand?'

'I have some skills in that area yes.'

'Some skills! I've read your bio, Dr Lane. He was trained by one of the elite Shadow Wolves, the Native Americans who patrol the borders of the US for drugs and people smugglers. Tell us what you saw on the ground at the site this morning.'

'It wasn't easy to read because so many had been in the field since its discovery, but I have no doubt that there was a group of people involved in the killing. This wasn't even a handful of people; I think we are looking at ten, perhaps even more.'

'Shit!' someone murmured.

'This is like some Wicker Man thing,' an older, female police detective said to the room.

'It's not quite the same,' Harrison replied, 'but it is certainly mob rule and not a couple of individuals conducting a crime.'

'Right, let's not go all horror movie about this,' Ross said to them all. 'This is a murder investigation and we need to stick to the facts and find out who is behind this. Oliver, you're leading on forensics; early days I know, but anything you can help us with?'

A man in his fifties rubbed his hands through his silvered hair and stood up to address the room. He looked down at his phone where he'd clearly jotted down some notes. 'Right, our victim is being taken down as we speak, we should have them in the autopsy room within the next hour or so. They're obviously badly burnt but the upper body in particular hasn't been completely destroyed so I'm confident we'll get DNA. I'm also confident, having been up closer, that we are talking about a female. Accelerant was used and the fire inspector said his bets were on diesel, but we can't confirm that just yet.

'We are looking into what could have created the furrows that Dr Lane mentioned to make the symbol, and we think some kind of vehicle with stabilisers was also used at the site to prepare the bonfire or the victim. I'd be looking for an access boom type of vehicle. Something to note is that the field gate was padlocked, and yet it looks like it was the only access. We're analysing the wood used in the bonfire. It appears to be a mixture of tree branches, chopped trees and what I'd call waste wood, such as old garden fence panels and wooden crates. That's the crime scene.' Oliver looked up from his notes and then carried on.

'Louise Swift's cottage is still being searched. You asked us to look for a laptop,' he said addressing Gibbons, 'but so far nothing I'm afraid. It's certainly not in the office area. We've not found any traces of blood yet but whoever was there was clearly looking for something. They thoroughly searched every inch of that office.'

Gibbons sighed. 'So no way of knowing if Louise was forcibly taken from her cottage?'

Oliver shook his head. 'Nothing that would indicate that yet. If there had been a struggle, the signs would have likely been obliterated by the ransacking.'

'What about the door to doors?'

A female detective spoke next, tucking her blonde hair behind her ears as she concentrated on what she was saying. 'We have spoken to almost everyone in the village. No one saw or heard anything. Nothing going on at Louise Swift's cottage and no noises from the fields.'

Gibbons shook his head in disbelief. 'And I suppose we still don't have any possible CCTV in a fifteen-mile radius?'

A room full of heads shook back at him.

'Right, then we keep digging. This wasn't a random crime, or a spur of the moment one. This required planning and logistics. Somebody must have noticed something over the previous weeks. I want a list of all Louise's clients. Her assistant said she had a desk diary. We need that found ASAP and every appointment checked. In the meantime, our biggest problem is going to be containing the legions of ghouls who have turned up to get a look, along with the TikTok amateur sleuths. They are a threat to this investigation by spreading misinformation and trampling all over our crime scene. Anyone caught in a restricted area is to be arrested. I need everyone to be vigilant and extra cautious. The superintendent is aware and is drafting in extra uniforms to manage the situation.'

'What about the protestors?' a uniformed sergeant asked.

'Protestors?'

'Yeah, there's a couple of groups arrived at the fire site. One lot are from a stop violence against women group and the others look to be like radical Christian types who are saying prayers and wanting to cleanse the area. We're keeping them apart at present, but I wouldn't put it past one of those social media vampires to try to stage an altercation between them, just to get some views.'

'We don't have the resources to babysit these people, our priority is the investigation. I'll talk to the superintendent and see if we can hold a media interview and ask them to all go home and allow us to do our jobs. He needs to be clear that we won't tolerate interference.'

'Yeah, some hope,' somebody in the room muttered.

'Listen, we have to focus on the inquiry. If it looks like it's going to get out of control, then maybe we can bring in some reinforcements from another force. This is national news so tight budgets or not, management know they have to deal with this or face criticism.'

Gibbons looked around the room.

'We've a job to do, let's not let a small minority of misinformed narcissists stop us. Thistleford is a small village, I want to know the names of every single one of the people who live there and I want every single one of their backgrounds checked. Where were they last night? Did they really not see or hear anything? Dr Lane and I are going up to Harmony House to get a feel for what kind of welcome we can expect there. Let's crack on and reconvene tomorrow morning first thing.'

EIGHT

Harmony House, formerly Blethen House according to the ancient road sign, was a large country estate, walled in and gated. Through the large wrought-iron gates, there was no sign of the house within, just a small wooden structure right in front that barred any vehicular access along the road.

'Well this is weird,' DS Gibbons said. Harrison had got a lift with him in his car so they could travel together. 'How do you go up to the main house with that in the way?'

'Perhaps that's the whole idea. You don't,' Harrison replied.

DS Gibbons made a grunt of dissatisfied agreement and got out of the car, crossing to the gate post where an entrance panel was situated. He pressed the button and nothing happened.

'I think it's dead,' he said to Harrison, who had wound down his window.

'Is that a bell pulley?' Harrison replied, pointing at a brass handle that appeared to be attached to a rope.

Gibbons reached for it and pulled. They heard a clang clang sounding in the wooden structure beyond the gates. A few moments later, a man walked out. He was dressed in simple clothes – a long shirt and loose trousers – which looked as though they were handmade and dyed. He also looked as if he'd just been sleeping and they'd rudely awoken him. He said nothing, just walked up to the gate and looked from Gibbons to Harrison.

'We want to speak to someone in charge please. I'm Detective Sergeant Ross Gibbons and this is Dr Harrison Lane.'

'Why?' came the gruff response.

'It's in connection to an incident that has occurred in a field that is rented by your group.'

'Wait,' was all he got in reply. The man retraced his steps and disappeared. With the wooden structure barring any view up the access road, there was no way of seeing if anyone was coming or going. All they could do was stand and wait.

For the first five minutes, Gibbons just tapped his foot impatiently, but the longer the time dragged on, the more agitated he got.

'What's he doing? Walking up to the house and back?'

'Probably,' Harrison said to him. 'I don't think they have any vehicles if that wooden building is anything to go by, and I didn't hear any kind of an engine start up.'

Rather than do nothing, Harrison used the time to look at the gates and surrounding walls. 'There doesn't seem to be any cameras or other security,' he said to Gibbons. 'Someone could probably scale the wall if they climbed that tree there.'

'Maybe, but don't go getting any ideas; we can't. For one thing we need to try to get their cooperation and secondly, we've no idea what's on the other side. They might have attack dogs or anything and we'd be trespassing.'

Instead, Gibbons pulled the bell again. Both of them listened to its clang clang and waited. The same man came to the gate.

'I've sent for Finn. He'll be here soon,' he said to them both, stony faced and clearly not impressed with their impatience. He didn't wait for them to reply, or stop to enjoy their company, he just turned and walked back.

Gibbons muttered something unintelligible – which Harrison presumed to be an expletive – and then started looking at his emails on his phone.

Ten minutes later, two men and the original gatekeeper approached them from behind the gates.

'Can we help you?' The oldest of the three, a man with long grey hair and beard, spoke first. There was something quite regal in the way he carried himself, and his hair and beard didn't look scruffy or unkempt.

'Detective Sergeant Gibbons.' The DS showed his warrant card. 'We wanted to talk to you about the field that you rent from Nick Rogers.'

'We wondered how long it would be before you were at our gates. It's nothing to do with us. Yes we rent the field, but what happened there is quite unrelated. We won't be requiring the field anymore now. It will be contaminated.'

'Sorry, you are?'

'Finn.'

'Finn—?' DS Gibbons queried, clearly asking for a surname and looking to the other two as well.

'As I'm sure you are well aware, detective, we are under no obligation to give you our names unless you believe we have committed an offence.'

'I'm not here to accuse you of anything, Finn, I'm just trying to find out who brutally murdered an individual on a field you rent.'

'Not us.'

'Look, can we come in? It would be a lot easier than talking through this gate.'

'If you don't mind we would prefer it if you didn't. You can't bring your vehicle in anyway. We don't allow cars or any motorised vehicles on our land because we

don't want any poisonous metals and other emissions cont-
aminating it.'

'Can I ask who *we* is?'

'We're a group of like-minded individuals who want to live
away from the toxicity of modern life. We're self-contained and
self-sufficient. We ask nothing from the outside world and ask
that the outside world leaves us alone.'

'Are you missing any members?' DS Gibbons asked.

'No.'

'When was the last time any of your commune visited the
field in question?'

'Yesterday afternoon a couple of them walked past. There
was nothing to see there.'

'No pile of wood?'

'No pile of wood.'

'Some of your members have been seen collecting wood
from around the area.'

'That is quite likely, yes. We don't have electricity or gas, we
derive our energy from natural sources, that means we have
wood fires, detective.'

'So you're the leader of this commune?'

'I am the elected spokesperson. We are run by a committee
which is voted on by all members. This is not a cult, detective, if
that's what you're asking. I don't dictate how we live and our
religious affinity is more akin to early Celts, in that we celebrate
the earth and the sun, not worship a single deity.'

'How many of you are there?'

'Sixteen.'

'How did you recruit people?'

'I didn't recruit anyone, detective, I was lucky enough to be
able to buy this property and to start living the kind of life that I
wanted to live. Others have just joined me because they wanted
to. Mostly it's through word of mouth, people knowing someone
else. They come because modern life has traumatised them,

some have PTSD, others just worn down by its relentless pressures.'

'Do you have any children among you?'

'No. All adults but what does this have to do with our field, detective?'

DS Gibbons avoided that question. 'The padlock on the gate into the field was still locked when we arrived on the scene. I presume you have the key?'

'We do. It's kept in the house. We have a place for all the keys so that everyone knows where they are when needed.'

'Could any of your residents have taken the key last night?'

'They could have but they didn't, detective. I saw the key last night, they're hanging up in the kitchen, and it was also there this morning.'

'But they could have taken it after everyone else went to bed?'

'Anything is possible but as I said to you, we had nothing to do with what went on in that field last night.'

'Do you know a Louise Swift?'

Finn shook his head and looked to the other two with him who both shook their heads.

'No.'

'We have a witness who said they saw Louise Swift arguing with a man matching your description.'

'Is this Louise Swift the victim in the field?'

'We don't know that but she appears to have gone missing.'

'We get confronted by the villagers and others that live around here occasionally, detective. They don't like us even though we have done nothing wrong. They accuse us of all sorts of things because they don't understand why we want to stay out of their society. I will say this for one last time, detective, this murder has nothing to do with us. We were all here last night. Now if you don't mind, we need to get back to work.'

With that, Finn and the other two men turned and walked

away from the gate, leaving Gibbons and Harrison standing staring at their backs.

'Well that was a bloody frustrating half hour, but then we did expect it,' Gibbons said as they got back in the car. He executed an aggressive three-point turn to get back onto the lane. 'That Finn fitted the description that Charley gave us about the man seen arguing with Louise, for sure.'

Harrison had said nothing throughout the conversation, preferring instead to watch and listen – or so he told himself. If he was really honest it had been more personal than that. He'd lived in communes as a child, his mother drifting from one place to another looking for spiritual guidance. Finn looked nothing like Desmond Manning, the man who had been in his night-mares for most of his life, until he'd finally tracked him down and arrested him a couple of years ago. Desmond and his wife, Freda, had used and terrorised people for their own gain, taking a person's insecurities and beliefs and twisting them to control them. It had been the catalyst for Harrison's career, but he had to be careful that he didn't allow his own personal experiences to cloud his judgement. There was no evidence to suggest that Finn was evil and the commune an unhappy place. Neverthe-less, he felt a shiver of relief when they drove away from the walled estate.

'Yes. He's an intelligent man, Finn, if that's what his name is,' Harrison said to Ross.

'We'll check with land registry. If he bought it then his name's going to be on the deeds. I'd like to know who else is in there with him. For all we know they could be psychopaths and criminals, that's what Nick Rogers seemed to suggest.'

Harrison said nothing further. The group were obvious suspects. Any individuals who shut themselves off from the rest of the world were bound to attract speculation. Question was whether it was justified or not, and for that Harrison would have to do a little of his own digging around.

NINE

It had been a long night and day. Tiring but satisfying.

As the sun sank below the skyline, a few of them gathered in the shadows to discuss the day's events.

'How's everyone holding up?' he asked them.

'Fine. All good,' they reassured him.

He looked at them all carefully. There was safety in numbers, but then again a chain was only as strong as its weakest link. If one of them broke, it could bring them all down.

'Anything else besides the laptop and her phone?'

Heads shook.

'Then destroy them. They're no use to us and if somehow, they're found, it would come back to bite us.'

All heads nodded.

'What about the media and the others who have come? They're going to start harassing us all.'

'You ignore them. They'll eventually lose interest. We just stick to the plan.' He saw the fear in the eyes of the questioner. 'We're fine. They'll get nowhere and neither will the police. There's nothing to worry about. The witch is dead and we will be able to get on with our lives now.'

He watched them as they melted away into the dark shadows of the night. There were a couple that he worried about – perhaps they could be swayed by guilt and remorse. He'd need to keep a close eye on them. If he thought for one moment that they might be too weak, then he'd have to deal with them. The safety of the group as a whole was far more important than one individual.

TEN

Harrison booked himself into a hotel in the town, near to the police station. He did contemplate riding back to Thistleford and getting a drink in the pub there – non-alcoholic of course, as he hadn't touched alcohol since just after his mother's death – but in the event he decided he was too tired. He went for a walk around the town just to get some air and exercise and to clear his mind.

It was an English market town, a mix of independent shops and chain retail outlets, and the usual proliferation of coffee shops. A group of rowdy teenage boys were walking along the high street, all showing off, shouting and trying to impress each other and whoever else was watching with their group masculinity. It was all false bravado that quickly evaporated as they approached Harrison. None of them wanted to antagonise him and get into a fight and so the energy of the group quickly fizzled and deflated into a more respectable group of lads just walking to the pub.

Harrison chose a small local restaurant for dinner. Picking some *clean food* as he called it, meat, veg, and some carbohydrate without any of the added ingredients of ultra-processed food. It was good. The veg was crisp and cooked perfectly and his steak medium rare, just as he liked it.

He thought about his morning and the empty wardrobe he'd built in his flat, and messaged Tanya.

> How's it going?

She started replying immediately but seemed to be taking forever to type it. Finally, her response came through.

> All good. Went out with Maxine and Jane after work. Talked about single nucleotide polymorphism loci for two hours. Shit, took me ten goes before spellcheck would let me write that! Latest DNA sampling technology.

Harrison smiled at the thought of her frustration trying to type the message, and at her passion for her job in forensics.

> How's it going with the case? Saw it on the news. Shocker

Very early stages

> OK, let me know when you're heading home and I can try out the new wardrobe x

Harrison realised he was smiling again at his phone and suddenly felt very far from home in the little restaurant. That was another thing he'd noticed in the last few months: his flat had come to feel more like a home than just a place to go and escape from the world. He hadn't yet decided if this *softening* in him was a good thing or not. Right now, all he knew was that he'd far rather be in his flat with Tanya by his side, than here alone in a strange town – but he had a job to do. A woman had been murdered and he needed to help bring her killers to justice. If there was a group who were so extreme that they would stone and then burn a person alive, then the chances are they wouldn't stop there. They had to be caught. He asked for the bill and walked back to his hotel.

Once he was inside his room, Harrison messaged Ryan to see how he was getting on with his research.

You free to call?

Harrison sent a thumbs up back and his phone immediately began a WhatsApp video call with Ryan. The slightly worried face of his assistant appeared.

'You alright, Ryan?' Harrison sat up concerned.

Ryan had been forced to move flats just last year when a drugs gang who knew about his special online talents had tried to kidnap him in order to secure his services for their business. While his agoraphobia meant he rarely went out, there was always the chance they'd tracked him down again.

'Yeah I'm fine, but I'm sorry, boss, that Harmony House lot are proving tough.'

'I thought they would be.'

'They're mega secretive. Totally off grid. Only thing I can find is that the purchaser of the property was Harmony House Collective, which is a company that has a Finn Smith as its only director. Nothing on who he is and where he came from at all. I'm going to check if he's changed his name or has a criminal record, but so far no past residents spilling stories, no idea of who is even living there. Been going about four years and seem to have been left to get on with things. Until now. A couple of social media posts have sprung up asking who they are and if they're involved in your witch murder.'

'I didn't think you'd find much. They said that they don't have electricity so I figured there wouldn't be an online presence. I'm going to have to go old school. Finn looks like an intelligent man so it doesn't surprise me that he's covered his tracks online, especially if he's got money. Be interesting to find out where that money came from.'

Ryan relaxed slightly. Harrison realised this was one of the first times that he'd not been able to give him a fully detailed report or find something juicy.

'Louise Swift was a lot easier. She's from Lewisham, Jack's stomping ground. All over the internet. Does online readings for people, telling them they're going to meet the partner of their dreams and come into money and all that crap.'

'Any criminal record?'

'Nothing that comes up apart from a shoplifting spree about ten years ago. She wasn't charged but was given a warning.'

'So, no fingerprints taken then?'

'Nothing on record, no. I'll send you all I've got on her with links to her TikTok and YouTube channels.'

'Thanks, Ryan.'

'I've looked into the village and the area too. There's no history of any witches around there, nothing special about that site, but...' Ryan raised his eyebrows and there was a twinkle in his eyes. This was more like the usual Ryan. 'I've found a small group who have aligned themselves to that fundamentalist Christian guy who was discredited in Australia, Howard Carter. They reckon he was framed and some of the things they say are pretty far out there.'

'That is interesting... and they're around here?'

'Yup, just the other side of Thistleford village to the Harmony House lot. It's only a small place so pretty under the radar, but I don't reckon they'd think much of someone who was a medium like that Louise Swift.'

'I'm familiar with the Logos Foundation and Howard Carter. They split from him and formed a new church when he was discredited, but if this is a splinter group that aligns with him, then they might be more radical.'

'I'll send you what I have,' Ryan said to him. 'They call themselves the Thistleford Community Church. They've turned an abandoned farm into their home and a barn is their church. There are images of them renovating it online. Women all wearing long dresses up to their necks carrying trays of food or sewing, the men doing the building work and clearly in charge.'

'I'll check them out, cheers, Ryan.'

Once they'd finished the call, Harrison crossed to the mini kettle in his room and filled it up from the tap. He had some of his favourite herbal tea that he always carried in his away bag and he made himself a mug before sitting down to watch Louise Swift. Getting to know his victim was critical. The more he could gauge who she was and what she had done in her life, the easier it would be to formulate an idea of who might wish her harm.

There was no way he was going to make an account with TikTok, so he browsed as a guest, following the link that Ryan had sent him.

In front of him, he recognised the office he'd seen earlier that day – only before it had been pulled apart. She had her camera set up so you couldn't see anything but mystic tarot imagery, with a wooden table carved into a hand with its palm facing upwards. Onto this she shuffled and placed cards.

'This video is timeless,' she said, smiling to camera. 'If you're watching this, it's because you were meant to see this. This is a message for you.' She shuffled the tarot cards and paused for dramatic effect. 'I can see that there's a spirit around you right now, a person in your life who is draining your energy. Their negativity is dragging you down. You deserve more than what they're giving you. Yes I hear you, you're finding it hard to move on. It's not easy, I know. I can see the pull of their energy but it's OK.' She shuffled and pulled another card from her deck, showing it to the camera and smiling into it. 'Just out of your view, there is another soul who is waiting for you. I see them. There is going to be some kind of heart-to-heart conversation you're going to have with this person and they're going to connect with you. They want you but they thought you were unobtainable, they saw the hold that the negative person in your life right now has over you. There is something they want to say but they're worried about the impact their words might have and that's because they care about you and because they don't think showing their feelings will be successful.'

She paused from her reading a moment and then stared into the camera lens. 'If you want to know how to encourage this person to speak up, what signs they are going to give you so that you know who they are, then let me know in the comments and be sure to watch part two.'

Harrison shook his head and swiped up for the next one on her timeline.

'If you're seeing this video, this message is for you. I know money is tight right now, but there are great things coming...'

He watched video after video, all of them trying to persuade people to sit for a private reading, which she charged for, and all of them praying on the every day worries and stresses that everyone has to varying degrees. Relationships, money, job, and ill health.

He looked at the woman in the videos, did she really believe what she was saying? That she had powers to help people? He's seen various clues in her cottage that hinted at something, but he'd need to go back there once forensics were finished to confirm his thoughts.

Did she record the private readings? Perhaps she'd upset somebody in one of them? Or maybe somebody or a group of people really believed in what she was saying and that she did have special powers, enough to want to silence her or to think her evil. Right now, the mode of murder seemed to suggest the latter as the most likely, and that hinted at some extreme views.

Harrison couldn't watch any more of her videos and so swiped away from her feed. He found himself being served cute dog and cat videos instead, which he watched for a couple of minutes before realising what he was doing and clicking away from the app. That was a place he didn't intend to go again. Louise Swift's cottage, however, was definitely on his 'need to revisit' list.

ELEVEN

Harrison got a text from DS Gibbons as he was eating breakfast.

> Autopsy underway, meet me at the hospital
> morgue 9 a.m.

He stopped chewing and looked at the plate of sausage, egg and bacon in front of him. Had he known where he was going, he might have made a different breakfast choice, but it was too late now. Harrison finished his food, looked up where he was going and set off on his bike for the hospital morgue.

DS Gibbons was just exiting the hospital café at the entrance when Harrison walked in.

'Dr Lane, I messaged you,' he said holding up two takeaway cups.

Harrison pulled out his phone. 'I was riding my bike. I don't drink coffee, but thanks,' he said.

'No worries, I usually have them lined up, need at least three to get me going in the morning.'

'And it's Harrison,' he added, keen to dismiss the formalities.

'OK, Ross too.'

The pair of them walked down a long corridor, swerving trollies, wheelchairs and people on crutches.

'Not sure how much this is going to tell us, apart from one key question, whether she was alive when they lit that fire. It's going to take a couple more days yet before we can have DNA confirmation for identity.'

Ross finished one cup of coffee by the time they were halfway down the corridor, and downed the last dregs of the second cup as they waited to be let into the autopsy area. Harrison noticed the detective didn't seem at all apprehensive about what they were about to see, unlike so many of Harrison's colleagues. He could think of a fair few who wouldn't have been able to drink two cups of coffee and then go to an autopsy without mishap.

They put on protective clothing to ensure the examination area and evidence didn't get contaminated, and were shown into the autopsy room where the pathologist was midway through the procedure.

The pathologist was a quietly spoken man of indeterminable age. He could have been an old-looking thirty-five, or a young-looking fifty-five. Even Harrison found it difficult to tell as most of the man was gloved and masked up and his hair covered in a protective hat.

'Morning, gents,' he said to them both, pausing with a scalpel mid-air.

'Bones,' DS Gibbons said, raising a hand to him. 'Dr Lane, this is Byron Eriksen, or Bones to his friends. How's it going?'

'Slowly. She's fragile – the fire has pretty much decimated her lower body but we do still have soft tissue up top. Most importantly, the lungs were in reasonable shape and so I'm afraid I can confirm she was alive when the fire was lit.'

Harrison saw the compassion in the eyes of the pathologist. They all knew that the blackened remains on the metal gurney table in front of them had once been a human being. There was no mistaking that. The air in the examination room was cooled and circulated by air conditioning, but it was nevertheless filled with the acrid charcoal stench of burnt flesh and organic matter.

'No hair left obviously, to help with identity,' the pathologist continued, 'but she was wearing a couple of rings. They're in a dish over there.'

Harrison and Ross crossed over to the dish and peered at the soot-blackened metal rings.

'They are the same two that Louise wore,' Harrison said, pulling out his phone and showing Ross an image that he'd taken from the TikTok videos last night. 'A silver witch's knot ring and one with three red stones: garnets or rubies. It raises the chance it's her.'

'Yes, it's looking increasingly like she's our victim. We've still not found any trace of her. However, she or someone else could have taken her rings and put them on the victim to make it look like her for some reason, so we're still going to have to wait until the DNA results to call it. Anything else you can tell us, Bones?' Ross Gibbons turned back to the pathologist.

'Mmhm, she certainly wouldn't have died immediately, although the pain and smoke inhalation might have mercifully made her unconscious, but I've seen no evidence of any kind of a gag. Now she could have been drugged; I'm not going to be able to tell you that until all the tests are done, but if she wasn't, she'd have been screaming for a while. A pretty harrowing way to kill someone unless you really hated them.'

'Or were afraid of them,' Harrison added.

Both men looked at him.

'Did you find any impact injuries on her?'

'Impact? What kind of thing are you thinking?'

'There were various rocks and stones around the bonfire which didn't look as though they were originally in the field.'

'So you think they stoned her?' Bones raised both his eyebrows above the face mask, and shook his head. 'If they were throwing the stones at her when she was already on the fire, then I suspect the velocity will have only resulted in soft tissue injuries. Those are likely to have been obliterated by the fire. But I've done a scan on her so I'll look for any small breaks or internal signs of injury. Realistically, I'm not sure I'm going to find much evidence of that though, not after the job the fire's done on her.'

Harrison nodded his head in sad agreement. 'Did you find any kind of religious symbolism on her?'

'No. The only jewellery was the rings. Clothing was mostly burnt away apart from some scraps on the tops of her shoulders. Didn't look unusual. She was chained to the cross. It's all gone for testing but I doubt you'll get much thanks to the fire. The chain was wrapped around her body several times with her hands and arms tied behind her. That way I guess ropes couldn't burn through and potentially release her. She had no chance.'

The three men stood in silence for a moment contemplating the pale pink and blackened remains in front of them.

'Were there any signs, that you can see, of torture? I appreciate that's not an easy ask,' Harrison queried.

'As I said, I put her through the scanner before I started the examination, that way we can see the state of her internal organs and bones before disturbing them. I need to look at those images again before I can be one hundred per cent, but I did a cursory look over and saw nothing to suggest any kind of trauma injuries into deep tissue and on bone. Yet again I'm afraid she may have been tortured, but the fire has obliterated the evidence. Sorry I can't be more helpful, but it's never easy with fire victims.'

'Of course,' DS Gibbons reassured him. 'We'll leave you to it. We need to crack on, there's a lot of people to speak to.'

. . .

Harrison and DS Gibbons left the mortuary, exiting into the brightly lit hospital corridor where they could leave the dead behind and return to the world of the living.

They walked silently back to the car park. Harrison wasn't the most talkative at the best of times, and he was quite happy that DS Gibbons seemed to need some quiet time too.

They'd just reached his car when Ross's mobile went off. Harrison watched as his face turned from deep thought to anger. 'I'll meet you there,' the DS said down the phone, ended the call and turned to Harrison.

'The crime scene is being overrun, they're having to bring in a riot squad. Would you believe they're taking pieces of the wood as souvenirs. Do you want to come?'

'Yes. It will be interesting to see who's there.'

'Absolutely, I know sometimes the killers return to the scene. But that's only if we can bloody well spot them in the crowd. Jump in, your bike will be fine here.'

Harrison got into the car and wondered what they were going to be driving into.

TWELVE

'Holy crap!' was DS Gibbons's reaction when they arrived on the lane that led to the bonfire field. It was jam-packed with people. Some had placards, others were chanting and some just had their mobile phones held aloft, presumably streaming live video of the chaos. 'This is one shitshow. What is with people? Why can't they let us get on with our jobs? I'm going to have to leave the car here, we can't risk pushing through and injuring someone.'

As they went to get out of the car, Harrison looked at the detective. He estimated that he was around six inches shorter than himself and had the build of a cyclist rather than a bodyguard.

'Just a suggestion, but you might want to let me go first.'

DS Gibbons turned to him and raised his eyebrows, then smiled. 'Happy to let you be my people plough,' he said. 'I'd certainly move if I saw you heading towards me and didn't know if you were friendly or not.'

Harrison gave a nod and the pair of them got out and joined the stream of people heading up the lane. DS Gibbons fell in behind him.

'Excuse me,' Harrison said as he gently carved his way through the crowd. Most of them took a double take and stepped back out the way, occasionally someone argued.

'Police. You shouldn't be here,' Harrison replied to them firmly. He'd never been a fan of rubberneckers and those who turned up at crime scenes just to get a look and preferably a selfie. One woman took offence and started saying it was typical of two men pushing their way through a crowd of women. She held a placard declaring she was against violence towards women and planted herself in front of them.

Harrison paused a moment to speak to her. 'This man is the detective who is trying to get justice for the woman who was murdered here and make sure her killer is put in prison. Do you really think that blocking our way is going to help her?'

She backed down with a mutter and they continued working their way through the crowd. Finally, they reached the field and what should have been the police *no entry* tape. It was trampled on the ground and there were no officers in sight.

DS Gibbons rushed on ahead into the field. Part of the forensic screen had been torn down and around half a dozen uniformed officers were trying to keep people away from the bonfire, helped by three fire officers. As soon as they stopped one person, another snatched at a piece of the wood, stealing it for souvenirs. Others were standing taking videos and selfies. A group of people were kneeling on the ground as though in prayer. There was a steady flow of new people pouring in off the lane.

Harrison quickly assessed the huge task in front of them. With so few people, it was going to be tough to bring things under control. The riot squad were on their way, but in the meantime, valuable evidence was being stolen and trampled on.

'Try to contain those in the field, I'm going to stop any more from entering,' Harrison shouted to DS Gibbons.

The gate to the field had been forced right back and so

Harrison grabbed it and began closing it, pushing people back into the lane. 'You can't come in here. It's a crime scene,' he shouted at them. He created enough of a shock factor for most of them to pause for a moment, but he had to use all his strength to push the gate closed, digging his feet into the ground and shoving with his thick thighs and broad shoulders, his biceps turning solid with the strain. Harrison didn't want to hurt anyone, but he was determined to shut the gate. Finally as it clicked shut into place, one guy decided he wasn't having any of it and started climbing over.

'Don't do that,' Harrison said, squaring up to him. 'You step one foot in this field and not only are you going to be arrested, but I'm going to have to forcibly restrain you. This is a crime scene.'

The guy let forth a string of expletives, some of which Harrison hadn't even heard before.

'You can't stop me. If you touch me it's going to be broadcast live to the world.' Behind him a row of phones were being held up as others filmed the altercation. He took another step up the gate, staring at Harrison, daring him to react and getting ready to swing his leg over.

'It should be broadcast, you are breaking the law and endangering a murder inquiry. I will give you one final warning,' Harrison said. 'If you attempt to come into this field then I am going to detain you for entering a restricted area and you will be arrested.'

'You don't look like a cop to me,' the bloke retaliated. Those around him were egging him on. They all wanted to get into the field, and failing that, they wanted a good bit of video to put on their social feeds. The man was fired up, his pupils dilated and cheeks flushed. Not letting his eyes leave Harrison's, he swung his leg over the top of the gate and then jumped down into the field.

Harrison shook his head. The man had just enough time to

turn up the corners of his mouth into a smug, defiant smile before his legs went out from underneath him and his face was firmly planted in the mud.

The crowd protested, shouting abuse, but Harrison didn't even break into a sweat as he pulled the trespasser back up and hitched his arms behind his back.

The man tried to wriggle from his grip, but made no headway. Harrison held on to him with one arm and stared defiantly at the crowd as though challenging them to try the same move.

'You'll need these,' DS Gibbons said, coming up behind Harrison, and held out a set of handcuffs. 'I'll read him his rights.' Then he looked up at the faces at the gate. 'Now, if any of you have any thoughts of coming into this field, then we will arrest every single one of you. This is a crime scene. I have specialist officers working to find out what happened here and who was involved. By trampling over the evidence and stealing parts of it, you are helping the killer or killers. Is that really what you want to do? Because I want justice for the woman who was killed here and I would hope that you do too.'

The crowd murmured and jostled, but none of them were brave enough to try to scale the gate.

When Harrison looked back towards the bonfire, he saw those who had already got into the field, all standing in a group with the uniformed officers collecting whatever it was that they'd stolen from the bonfire. Of course, they had no way of knowing how much had already been taken. No doubt it would soon be appearing on eBay as ghoulish souvenirs or spiritual talismans. The victim would be a martyr in the eyes of those who practised Wicca, an indication that the prejudices that existed centuries ago are still alive today.

A few moments later, the sound of sirens coming up the lane caused the crowd to surge and then thin. A van of riot police arrived, followed by other officers and crowd barriers. Within twenty minutes the lane had returned to organised calm and all of those in the field had been sent on their way, apart from the man who'd climbed the gate who was instead about to be taken off to the nearest holding cell in the back of a police van. Two women who had received minor injuries from being crushed in the crowd and pushed into the hedgerow were being treated by paramedics.

The gate climber sneered at Harrison as he was taken away, but with the dirt on his face, there was little chance he could look remotely threatening.

'We probably won't charge him but I want him to think twice before he does that again. Thanks for your help,' DS Gibbons said to Harrison as they watched him being loaded into a holding van.

Harrison turned back to look at the field.

'What's the effect on the investigation likely to be?' He nodded towards the bonfire where the forensic fire officers were attempting to secure the evidence that was left.

'We could have lost some vital evidence. They've been logging all the wood to see if we can trace where it's come from. It's also going to play into the hands of any defence lawyer. Anything we get from the scene now could be so contaminated that it won't be admissible in court. Anyone could have placed something there or cross-contaminated. Why don't people think first? With all the cop shows and documentaries on TV, they know how important it is to preserve evidence.'

'Unfortunately this is no ordinary crime.'

'You can say that again.'

'When crimes like this happen, they can attain a spiritual or mystical status that either frightens people or bizarrely, reassures them. Has evil or good triumphed? That's what they want to know, because the reality of it being just a horrific way for one human to kill another, is far worse to contemplate.'

'Well I'm under no illusions,' replied Gibbons. 'This was a

murder committed by a bunch of evil-minded people and I want to find out who.'

While the crowds had fallen back from the field gate, there were still plenty of people in the lane behind the police barriers.

'I'm just going to take a look at who's here,' Harrison said to Gibbons, who was talking to one of the forensic team.

He turned right out of the gate this time, a direction he hadn't walked along, interested to see if there were different groups of people there. The majority of those he saw were just there for the novelty of the occasion. There were a few with placards, demonstrating against the violence, or the persecution of Wicca, but the atmosphere was like he'd expect at a carnival. He saw little genuine respect for the victim.

Harrison was about to turn back when he spotted a couple walking through the crowds handing out leaflets and trying to engage people in conversation. Were they selling something? Harrison didn't think it was goods or services. Some people threw their leaflets on the ground or looked as though they were being rude back to them. But the pair carried on unfazed by their reactions. The woman caught his eye and immediately they walked over.

'Hi,' she said, smiling sweetly at him. She was dressed as if she was about twenty or thirty years older than her age, no make-up on, and her hair was pulled back from her face. 'We're offering support to anyone upset about this evil event in our community.'

'Support?'

'Yes, brother,' the man addressed him now, and instantly Harrison recognised the language of a religious group. 'Our doors are always open, you can come along and share your fears and concerns with God.'

The woman held a leaflet out to him and Harrison spotted the logo of the Thistleford Community Church.

'Thanks,' he said to her. 'When do you meet?'

'This evening, friend, come and join us.' The man beamed back at him.

This was Harrison's opportunity to find out more about the Thistleford Community Church and he was definitely not going to miss this chance.

'Sure. I'll be there,' Harrison replied, pocketing the leaflet.

'Praise be, we look forward to welcoming you to our church, brother,' the man continued. 'Come with an open heart and mind and we will lead you towards healing and salvation.'

Harrison looked into the eyes of a man whose soul burnt with the passion of his belief. But was it a belief that was capable of thinking they were righteous in murdering a woman as a witch? That was a question Harrison hoped he might find the answer to that evening.

THIRTEEN

Harrison had already told DS Gibbons what Ryan had shared last night, and when he returned to the detective with the leaflet, his interest was piqued even more.

'You think they could have acted as the hand of God and killed her? It fits with the biblical stoning.'

'It's possible,' Harrison replied, 'but very risky and it would be interesting to see if she had any other dealings with them.'

'Well, chances are they're going to be about as cooperative as that lot at Harmony House and so if we can't find anything that links them, we're going to have a tough job finding anything out.'

'They've got a meeting tonight, invited me along, so I think I'll do just that,' Harrison replied.

'Well keep me informed in case there's any trouble – and it's strictly observation, we don't want to get accused of targeting them because of their religious beliefs. I can't be doing with all that paperwork.'

'I'll be fine,' Harrison replied earnestly.

'The office just rang. Apparently Louise Swift rented her cottage from Nick Rogers, who as we know, also happens to own this field. The other interesting fact is that three months ago she stopped paying him rent.'

'Blackmail?' Harrison wondered out loud.

'Or some other kind of favours for payment, maybe. He's not got a wife. They could have been having a relationship.'

'I can't see her being his type.' Harrison frowned.

'Sex is sex, Dr Lane. You don't have to take them to meet the parents or be seen out in public.'

'True.'

'Let's go pay him a visit and see what he has to say about the subject. Louise and his relationship, that is, not sex,' DS Gibbons clarified unnecessarily.

Harrison allowed himself a smile at his back and followed him down the lane. The atmosphere in the crowd, particularly further down the road, had eased from the anxious frenzy of earlier and now felt more like a quiet wake. Some groups had settled down for either meditation or prayers, and others were joining them, keen to experience this 'moment'. Harrison wondered just how much any of them were genuinely thinking about the woman whose remains he'd seen earlier in the morgue, rather than treating it like some kind of pop-up festival.

They saw Nick Rogers, or at least his silhouette, hovering in one of the downstairs windows as they pulled up the side entrance to his house. The village was busier than yesterday, with people taking photographs and selfies, or doing videos outside Louise Swift's cottage where a police squad car was parked and a uniformed officer stood guard at the front door.

As Harrison and Ross Gibbons stepped up to the Rogers's entranceway, the black gloss front door was pulled open and he waved them in.

'Quickly, I don't want anyone taking photographs,' he said to them, peering around his garden as though expecting to see someone hiding in the bushes. 'You know this is quite ridiculous. We're under siege. What are you doing about it?' He rounded on them both.

'We've drafted in extra colleagues to help us and we are arresting anyone who gets in the way of our investigation.'

'What about all that lot who were up in the field? I heard it got worse after I'd left. Complete chaos.'

'That is now under control and we will have officers there twenty-four seven.'

Nick Rogers snorted in a way which suggested he didn't believe that would make a difference.

'Do you know we've had people knocking on our doors wanting to do interviews with us for that TikTok app or some YouTube channel. It's invasion of privacy.'

'If anyone is bothering you then please call it in to us and we will deal with it. I'm fully aware that there are certain individuals who travel around the country from crime scene to crime scene, getting in the way of investigations and potentially endangering them. I won't tolerate interference here. Anyway, Mr Rogers, we wanted to just ask a few questions if that's OK?'

The conversation had taken place in the hallway, a neat classic style entrance that was exactly as Harrison would have imagined Roger's home to look. It was a stylish facade, polished and gleaming. What Harrison wanted to know was what was behind that facade. What made Nick Rogers tick.

'Come on through,' Rogers said, and led them into a neat traditional sitting room area, where the only real signs of a modern world was the large flat screen TV on the wall. All three of them sat down.

'We only spoke briefly yesterday and so we wanted to ask you a few more questions,' DS Gibbons began. 'As I'm sure you're aware, we don't yet have an identity for the victim, but clearly we are very concerned for Louise Swift and her whereabouts. Are you aware that her cottage has been ransacked and she is missing?' Gibbons paused to watch Nick Rogers's reaction and allow him to speak.

His face creased into concern. 'I am aware, detective. The whole village is in shock, and if I'm honest, also a little bit frightened by it all. We don't want to believe that the person in the field could be Louise, and yet I can see that there is a connection.'

Harrison concentrated on his face, watching for the emotional giveaways that would tell him what Nick Rogers was thinking.

'A connection, Mr Rogers?'

'Well, yes, that obviously Louise has gone missing and she is a very talented medium and spiritualist. I suspect that some people would see that as a form of witchcraft. I hasten to say that's not my view or anyone in the village. She was a very valued member of our community.'

'Any people in particular?' Gibbons tried.

'There's that lot up at Harmony House. No idea what they get up to.'

'But you rented them your field.'

'Well, yes, that's business and they said it was just for growing food. I had no idea that this was going to happen. There's also that group who call themselves the Thistleford Community Church. I wasn't happy when they turned up here. Taking our village name and using it for their radical views. My great-grandfather established this village, built this house and a lot of the cottages. He farmed the land around here and put his workers up in the cottages. We made this village.'

'There's no other church in the village?' Gibbons queried.

'No, we go to the one at Mountford. Our little community was too small to support its own congregation.'

'Do you know if Louise or anyone else in the village had any dealings with the Thistleford Community Church?'

Rogers shook his head and frowned. 'I visited them when

they first came here and told them I wasn't happy about them using the Thistleford name and their solicitor sent me a letter telling me not to harass them again and that they were legally entitled to call their church that.'

'No dealings since?'

'I definitely haven't and I'm pretty sure that nobody else in the village has anything to do with them. Those who still worship regularly go to Mountford church.'

'We understand that Louise Swift was your tenant?'

'Yes. I still own over half the cottages in the village.'

'So you own the field and you own her cottage,' Gibbons pushed without asking anything overtly.

'Yes.'

'Can you explain to me then why she hasn't paid you any rent in the last three months?'

Harrison watched Nick's body language. There was no nervousness.

'How would you know that? You've not been looking at my bank accounts, have you? I'll have to talk to my solicitor if you have.' He frowned at them.

'No, Mr Rogers. We have been looking at the victim's bank accounts and while we can see that she'd been regularly paying you a sum each month, that stopped three months ago.'

'So I'm now a suspect just because I showed a little bit of human compassion, am I?' He sat up straighter, defensive.

'I did not say that, Mr Rogers, I'm merely enquiring why? Were you in a relationship with Ms Swift?'

Rogers guffawed. 'Are you kidding me? No. She wasn't my type. She just had cash flow issues so I cut her some slack. She was a very gifted woman and she promised to pay me back. I believed her. But I guess now I'm not going to be seeing that money.'

'We don't know that yet, Mr Rogers. As I said, there is no confirmation that Louise is the victim from the field.'

'Well, let's hope not then.'

'So you gave her three months' rent free just because she was having cash flow issues?'

'Yes. Like I said, we're a small community here, detective, we look out for each other.'

'But Louise Swift wasn't really a part of this community, was she? She'd only been here two years.'

'She was relatively new, yes, but she'd thrown herself into village life. We don't just let anybody rent the cottages, you know. Anyone who wants to come and live here has to meet our village committee first to be approved. The last thing a tiny place like this needs is someone who will be disruptive.'

'Was Miss Swift disruptive in any way?'

'No. I told you. She was a much appreciated member of our community. She fully involved herself in village life.'

'In what way?'

'Well, you know…'

'No, Mr Rogers, I don't, can you please explain.'

Harrison could see a slight twitch on Nick Roger's face as DS Gibbons pushed him.

'She used to go into The Arms most days, everyone knew her. She was very talented, she helped lots of people and would always make herself available.'

'So, she used to go to the pub most days and talked to people, but what else made her a part of this community that you would trust a newcomer so much that you'd let them live rent free for three months?'

'You know I don't know what you're trying to get at, but I don't like your insinuation.' Nick Rogers glared at DS Gibbons and looked the wrong side of indignant. 'I don't know what you think might have gone on, but I've got nothing to hide.'

'Is there no Mrs Rogers?' Gibbons asked now.

'No. Not anymore,' Rogers replied curtly.

'Divorced?'

'No, detective. She took her own life.'

'I'm sorry to hear that.'

'Are you? What does my private life have to do with what happened up there in that field?'

'Did you ever have a reading with Louise?' Harrison asked now, attempting to break the tension that had built between the two men.

Nick Rogers switched his eyes to Harrison's and hesitated. He was clearly thinking through what to say and Harrison could see the animosity in his eyes.

'Most of us did. She'd do them in the pub and many people went for a private session too.'

'What kind of things did she tell you?'

'I'm not sure that's any of your business, it's not relevant and it was personal. I can't say all that was my cup of tea – I was sceptical at first, but she seemed to be really talented and was able to connect with people.'

'Did anybody get upset by any of her sessions?'

'No, I'd say she helped, gave people some hope.'

'Do you have a key to Ms Swift's cottage, Mr Rogers?' DS Gibbons asked.

'Of course. Oh, for—' he muttered an expletive under his breath and his eyes turned darker again; his pupils dilating with the anger he was clearly feeling. 'Yes. It's my cottage. I have a spare key. Sometimes tenants lose their keys. Sometimes I have to go in to get things fixed. I did not go into Louise Swift's cottage once without being invited and I certainly didn't go in there the night that all this kicked off. OK?'

'What about after?'

'After? No. Why would I? How could I? You've had a police officer there.'

'That's fine, Mr Rogers, it was just a question.' Gibbons smiled at him reassuringly, but it didn't look to Harrison as though that had appeased Nick Rogers any.

'Did you know if Miss Swift was worried about anything, or moved here to get away from a situation or somebody?'

Nick scowled, looking away as if for inspiration. 'Nothing that I'm aware of. I mean it's not like we had heart-to-hearts every day.'

'But didn't you ask for references before you rented the cottage to her?'

'I did yes. They seemed to be all in order.'

'Did she ever mention any family?'

He shook his head. 'I can show you her file if that helps you, but now you mention it, we knew very little about her life before she came here. She was very good at giving us information about ourselves, but didn't really share much about herself.'

'If you could show us what you have that would be useful.'

Nick got up and left the room without another word. Harrison heard him go upstairs and then a door opening and footsteps faintly above their heads. A minute later he was back with a brown cardboard folder.

'Here you can have it. It's of no use to me now,' he said handing the file to DS Gibbons. 'I hope you're asking that lot at Harmony House and the Community Church as many questions as you're asking us. They're the outcasts and extremists, if you're looking for a bunch of killers then they're your prime target.'

'We have spoken to a representative from Harmony House, but they've denied any knowledge of Louise and her murder.'

'You are kidding, right? Of course they would deny it. Have you gone through those gates? Seen what's really going on in there?'

'It's not easy to just enter a private property without any good reason, Mr Rogers, but I can assure you that we are being thorough in our enquiries...'

'Why don't you get a search warrant or something? Anything could be going on in there.'

'As I said, Mr Rogers, we can't just march onto a property without just cause. Can I just pick up on what you said about the Community Church, you called them "extremists". What has given you that view of them?'

'Have you looked into them at all?' Nick Rogers looked disdainfully at Gibbons. 'I consider myself a Christian, detective. I may not go to church every week, but even the vicar at Mountford has called their practices extreme. All this brother and sister stuff, I can tell you they're not into gender equality and the man they call *The Preacher*, well he looks like something from the dark ages. It's a cult, not a Christian church, I'm telling you. It's going to take some mass suicide or another extreme event before you authorities listen up and properly investigate. Too afraid of being accused of persecution these days, that's the problem.'

'I assure you, we are looking into all avenues of enquiry, Mr Rogers. Thank you for your information. Please remember though, that we still haven't had it confirmed who the victim is and so we aren't assuming it is Louise Swift. If she gets in touch with you or anyone else, you must let us know immediately.'

Nick gave a small tip of his head in response.

They left shortly after.

'Bit touchy wouldn't you say?' Gibbons said to Harrison as they shut the car doors.

'Just a bit, and what I find really interesting is that he says he cared enough about Louise Swift to allow her to live rent free for three months, and yet I've not seen any expression of grief or sadness at her possible murder. He talked about her in the past tense throughout. I'd say he's got a narcissistic personality from what I've seen of his behaviour so far: arrogant, likes to be the big man in charge, a definite sense of self-importance. He's the big fish in this small pond. I don't see him exhibiting the kind of empathy that would make him forego three months' rent. The question therefore is why did he really let her live rent free, and is he capable of murder?'

'Exactly my thoughts,' Gibbons echoed. 'But it's also interesting what he said about the Community Church, do you want someone to go with you tonight?'

'That won't be necessary. I have encountered many groups like this, and they aren't expecting anyone else. In my experience, they'd be able to spot a police officer a mile off.'

'Mmh, you're probably right. At least give me a call once you've left so it puts my mind at rest, would you?'

Harrison saw the father in DS Gibbons again and a brief memory of his own stepfather, Joe, came into his mind, along with a twinge of longing. It had been too long since he'd seen him. More worrying was that something else also curled into the back of his subconscious, a black snaking tendril that prodded at his childhood memories and reawakened fears he had hoped were long buried.

FOURTEEN

After they'd left Nick Rogers, Harrison and DS Gibbons returned to Louise Swift's cottage.

'I want to see if they've found that diary of hers Charley mentioned,' Gibbons said to Harrison. 'And have a chat with her neighbours. Can you really believe that nobody saw or heard a thing?'

'If she is our victim, then she could have met her killers someplace else and it's possible that nobody noticed someone returning to her cottage at night to look for whatever it was they were after,' Harrison said to him.

'Yes you're right, which is why that diary is so important. We've also not found her mobile phone, or her laptop yet.'

As they reached the front door to Louise's cottage, a small group of people took out their phones to take photographs or film them. Harrison angled his back to their lenses. He hated being in the public eye, much preferring as low a profile as possible. DS Gibbons muttered something unintelligible under his breath before talking to the officer on the door, who didn't seem to mind being the centre of attention.

'I know Oliver doesn't want us going in just yet, but is he or one of the other forensics team in there?'

'Yes, sir, I'll get him for you.'

'What's happening with the investigation? Why haven't you got any suspects?' A voice shouted at them. Neither Harrison nor Gibbons took any notice of them. Harrison's attention had been drawn by a man and woman further down the street who were being interviewed by a TV camera crew. They were clearly gushing about Louise as their faces were earnest and she had her hand on her heart. He made a mental note to turn the TV on in his hotel room to watch that later. The words that people used to describe someone and their body language weren't always in unison and could carry hidden messages. He wasn't surprised to see that the media had put two and two together and linked Louise's disappearance to the victim in the field. It was a logical conclusion but Harrison would welcome some scientific evidence to confirm that theory.

'They've found the diary.' DS Gibbons walked up to Harrison. 'No phone or computer, but you'll not guess what was written in her appointments for the afternoon she died.'

Harrison didn't try to guess and wasn't sure if DS Gibbons seriously intended him to, so he just waited.

'Harmony House.'

'Interesting,' Harrison said thoughtfully.

'Isn't it just. And Finn told us he didn't know her and she had nothing to do with them. Whoever ransacked the place must have taken her phone and computer, which suggests that there was evidence on there they didn't want us seeing. The good news is that I've got a name for a client she saw the day before. A Mrs Enid Wilson. Lives in town, not too far from the station. We can pop in to see her on the way back. At least see if she can give us an idea of Louise's state of mind.'

'I'd quite like to talk to some of the other villagers too, get a feel for them,' Harrison replied.

'Good idea. Nick Rogers and Charley Jones are two different ends of the spectrum. Would be nice to see what's in between. Let's start with the next-door neighbour as we're here.' DS Gibbons turned and knocked on the cottage door nearest to them. There was no reply.

He knocked again.

'I think they're all out, sir,' the officer on guard duty said to him.

'Who lives here?'

'The Burrows, mum and dad and their little one. Saw 'em going out earlier.'

'OK, thanks. What about on the other side?'

'Mrs O'Neil, she's in.' Then he mouthed so that nobody could hear, 'She's quite old.'

DS Gibbons thanked him and turned his attention to the cottage on the other side of Louise Swift's. 'Mrs O'Neil, it's the police. I wonder if we could have a word? Nothing to worry about, I just wanted to talk to you about Louise,' DS Gibbons spoke to the closed door, attempting to reassure the elderly woman inside.

There was no answer.

He knocked again. 'Mrs O'Neil, can you hear me? It's Detective Sergeant Gibbons, I'm investigating the disappearance of Louise Swift.'

A few moments later they were rewarded by the sound of a lock being scraped back and eventually the door creaked open a few inches. A wrinkled face with pale eyes and grey hair peered out at them.

'I've spoken to you already,' she said.

'Good morning, Mrs O'Neil, I believe you have spoken to my colleagues, I wonder if you wouldn't mind talking to myself and Dr Harrison Lane. We just wanted to ask you about Louise.' DS Gibbons showed her his ID.

'Nice girl she is,' the elderly woman replied. 'Where's she

gone then? I haven't seen her for a couple of days.' DS Gibbons shot Harrison a raised eyebrow as Mrs O'Neil opened the door to let them in. They followed her bowed back to a small sitting room that was a carbon copy of Louise's next door, apart from the decor. Mrs O'Neil clearly had a penchant for Royal Doulton figurines, which lined the walls on shelves and in cabinets. The furniture was also of a style befitting of her age and she had a small electric heater on which made the place feel more like a sauna than a sitting room.

'This is a lovely cottage, Mrs O'Neil. What a wonderful collection you have. My mother was a Royal Doulton fan.' DS Gibbons smiled and looked around at the shelves of figurines.

The old lady smiled back. 'Thank you. They're a bugger to dust though. My Mark is forever telling me to sell them, but I like them.'

'Mark is your—?' DS Gibbons left a pause for her to fill.

'My son. He lives just a few cottages up with his Stephanie. Not come up with any grandchildren yet but I live in hope.'

'How long have you lived in the village, Mrs O'Neil?'

'Violet. Everyone calls me Violet. Nigh on forty years now. Moved here with my husband. He used to work for the Rogers. Been gone a while now.'

'I'm sorry to hear that,' Gibbons replied. 'So you were already here when Louise moved in next door?'

'Ay, yes. Friendly lass she is.'

'Did Louise tell you anything about why she moved here?'

Violet frowned. 'Said she didn't get on with her mum, and her dad was nowhere around when she was growing up. Had a man who she was in love with, but he'd emigrated. Said she wanted a fresh start.'

'Did she ever say that she was scared of someone or trying to run away from something?'

'No. Always seems confident. I guess that's helped by her

talent. She's a very good clairvoyant, you know. Helped me talk to my Victor.'

'Your husband?'

Violet nodded.

'Did you see Louise regularly?'

'A few times a week. She pops in every now and then for a cuppa and a natter. I think she enjoys the company as much as I do.'

'And the last few times you've seen her, did she appear to be concerned about anything?'

Violet shook her head and appeared to think. 'No, nothing other than the usual. She struggles a bit with money.'

'She told you that?'

'Yes. I lent her a bit, just to tide her over.'

'Do you know how much you lent her, Violet?'

'I don't know now. Wrote it down in my cheque book. It's in that drawer over there. I don't have my glasses, but you can take a look.'

'Thank you,' DS Gibbons said, getting up and crossing to the drawer that she'd indicated.

While he looked in the cheque book, Harrison asked a few questions.

'Violet, you said Louise got in contact with your husband for you, did she do that regularly?'

'When he wanted to say something usually. She'd just come round and tell me he had got in touch with her and wanted to talk.'

'And if you don't mind me asking, did she charge for those sessions?'

'She never asked for anything. I used to give her some money and she'd try to refuse it, but I'd not take no for an answer. You're a big fellow, aren't you!' she suddenly added, looking at Harrison.

He smiled back at her. 'Yes, I'm quite tall. I don't suppose you noticed Louise practising any other kind of witchcraft or rituals, did you?'

'Witchcraft, what on earth are you saying? Louise isn't a witch.'

Just then they all stopped at the sound of a key going into the front door lock. A few moments later, a man in his forties, with a clearly increasing bald patch on the top of his head, walked into the sitting room.

'Mum, you alright?'

'Hello, love. This is my Mark I was telling you about,' Violet said to Harrison and DS Gibbons.

'Detective Sergeant Gibbons – and this is my colleague, Dr Harrison Lane.' Gibbons stepped forward offering his hand to shake.

Mark took it briefly.

'You know my mum can get a bit confused these days, so I hope you're not tiring her out.'

'I'm fine,' Violet said to him.

'We were just asking your mother about Louise Swift. Do you know her well?' DS Gibbons asked him, going to sit back down again.

Mark remained standing, moving closer to his mother. To Harrison, his body language was highly defensive. He stood rigid, as though ready to defend her.

'Yes, of course. We're only a small village here, you know. We all knew Louise.'

'Lovely girl, isn't she,' his mum said, smiling up at him.

'Were you aware that your mother lent Louise some money?' DS Gibbons asked.

'I am,' Mark confirmed, jutting his chin out defiantly. 'Louise used to sit with mum and gave her great comfort, letting her talk to my father.'

'Did you ever talk to your father through Louise?' Harrison asked now.

Mark shook his head. 'No. I left that to Mum.'

'What about any other kind of sessions?'

Mark stared at him, hard, for a moment. 'I asked her advice about a few things. She was able to give me some direction in how I should deal with some issues.'

'And did you ever get the impression that she was worried about anything herself?' DS Gibbons questioned.

Mark shook his head. 'No. She was happy here.'

'What about a couple of nights ago, Violet? Did you see or hear anything unusual at Louise's cottage?'

Mrs O'Neil shook her head. 'No, nothing unusual.'

'Did Louise get any visitors?'

'There are always people popping in and out, but I couldn't say who. I just hear the door opening and closing and shadows go by the window there.' Violet nodded to her sitting room window which looked out onto the street. It had thick net curtains hanging in it which obscured a clear view of outside.

'You didn't hear raised voices a couple of nights ago?'

'No, they are quiet. Even when they all came round together, they were quiet.'

'All came round together?' DS Gibbons queried.

'Yes. A group of them, I saw them all go past.'

'Mum, when did this happen? Are you sure you're not getting confused with another time? The detectives want to know about Tuesday night.'

'Tuesday! Oh I don't know about Tuesday. What day is it today?'

'It's Thursday Violet, but you can tell us about the group who visited Louise, it's OK. What happened?'

Violet's face seemed to go blank and she shook her head. 'Is she alright, Louise? I'm not sure what's going on and people keep asking me all these questions about her.'

She began to look upset and looked to her son for reassurance.

'It's alright, Mum, I'll explain it to you later,' he said to her quietly, resting his hand on her shoulder. Her hand went on top of his instinctively. 'I think that's probably enough for now, isn't it?' he said forcibly to Gibbons and Harrison.

'Yes, of course. Thank you for your time, Violet, it's much appreciated.' DS Gibbons rose from his chair.

'I'll see you out,' Mark said to them. 'Won't be a minute, Mum, I'll be back.'

He closed the door to the sitting room as they left and went into the hallway.

'My mum has dementia, she doesn't like leaving the cottage and gets easily confused. She doesn't know one day from the next so I honestly wouldn't give too much weight to what she tells you. She's probably referring to all those gawkers out there. Some of them have tried to knock on her door to speak to her. We are having to be very vigilant. If you want to talk to her again then can you let me know, as it helps when I'm here to reassure her. I don't want her getting upset.'

DS Gibbons smiled at Mark. 'Yes of course, Mr O'Neil. Can I ask, were you aware that your mother was giving Louise so much money?'

'As I said, I was aware that she was giving her money, yes. She brought my father back to her. What price do you put on a gift like that, detective? Louise wasn't like you and me, she was special.'

'But it was a substantial sum, Mr O'Neil, more than you would have expected a medium to charge.'

'My mother lent Louise some money; I believe that she was having some cash flow issues. It's my mother's affairs, Detective Gibbons, she worked hard all her life and earned that money so she could spend it on what she wanted. I fully support her in that.'

'Well that's very generous of your family. I'd have thought

what must have been close to ten thousand pounds in the last year would have caused some concerns?'

'Some concerns?' Mark was already tense, but his face turned rigid. 'We look after our own here, detective, if Louise needed the money then it was very kind of my mother to help her.'

'I keep hearing this comment, we look after our own and how close-knit this village is, and yet nobody saw or heard a thing on the night that one of your own disappeared and some-body was burnt to death in a nearby field. Doesn't that seem a little odd to you, Mr O'Neil?'

'We are all shocked and you're right, we feel like we let Louise down. So does that mean you've confirmed it was Louise who was killed? We've been hoping that it was a coincidence. Her talents had become well known in the local area. I appreciate that some people might not be as welcoming of her skillset as we were.'

'We haven't yet confirmed the identity of the victim, Mr O'Neil, and are keeping an open mind, but obviously we are very concerned for the welfare of Louise Swift.'

'As are we, detective. And I can assure you that if there is anything we can do to help catch her killers, then we will.'

Harrison and DS Gibbons stepped back out into the bright spring day and walked to Gibbons's car.

'Another one who talks about Louise in the past tense. He even said about catching her killers. Either they've all just convinced themselves that it was Louise in that field, or they know something for sure that we don't,' DS Gibbons said as he clambered into his car.

'And I don't care how bloody perfect they try to make their village seem, there's something about this place that gives me the creeps. They're all in each other's pockets and Rogers heads this all up. If Violet was my mother and she'd given ten thou-sand pounds to a medium while suffering from dementia, then I sure as hell wouldn't be happy about it, and that's just what we know so far that she got out of her. Can they really have been so taken in by her that they let her get away with all this?'

'I think that they were, certainly initially, yes,' Harrison replied.

'In that case, I wonder who else Louise was fleecing, because I can lay a bet there were plenty of others. If she was so broke then how would she have been able to afford to pay Charley Jones to help her? The more I get to know about Louise Swift, the more I can see the potential for some individuals who aren't as accommodating as the villagers appear. We need to look more closely at her bank account. She'd have had enemies alright, but why burn her at the stake like that? If it was just a revenge killing then surely they'd just do it and be done with it. Why make such a spectacle of it? Draw attention to her and her so-called gift? I think we have to look further afield than just this village, and further back in time to see what led her here.'

FIFTEEN

On the way back to the station, DS Gibbons and Harrison went round to see Enid Wilson, the woman that Louise had been to see the day before she disappeared. Mrs Wilson lived in a terraced house along one of the wide streets that were on the outskirts of the town. Built in the 1960s, they were solid and functional and boasted both front and back gardens, testament to the greater availability of space. Harrison suspected that these had all once been council-owned houses which over the years had been sold off at heavily reduced prices to their tenants. Now their investments were likely worth fifty times or more what they'd paid for them.

Enid Wilson opened the door to them both looking drawn and tired, an equally old-looking French bulldog was at her ankles. The dog had clearly decided it should still protect its mistress and territory, but the effort of getting up and going to the door had been quite enough.

'Do come in,' she said with a wavering voice. 'I'm sorry things aren't as tidy as they should be. We only buried my Tony two weeks ago and I've not quite caught up with things. Come on, Felix, out from under our feet.' The latter comment she aimed at the dog.

'We are sorry for your loss, Mrs Wilson,' DS Gibbons said.

'Will you be wanting a cup of tea?' she asked in response.

Harrison suspected that she was still struggling to accept peoples' condolences, still in a period of denial despite the reality around her.

'We're fine, thank you, we won't take up much of your time. We just wanted to ask you about Louise Swift?'

'Ah, yes.' Enid gave a small smile and settled into a chair next to a dog bed which was also quickly occupied.

'How did you get in touch with Ms Swift, was it online?'

'Online? Oh no I can't be bothered with all that. No, I didn't get in touch with her at all. She found me.'

'She found you?'

'Yes. It was on one of our strolls,' she said, looking down at her dog. 'We don't go far these days, but Louise was walking to go and see a friend and just stopped me and said that Tony had a message for me. Just like that.'

'Had you never met her before?'

'Never. She didn't know me at all. She said as she approached me she got the message from Tony and had to share it with me. It was him, I knew the minute she said it.'

'Do you mind me asking what the message was, Mrs Wilson?'

Enid Wilson's pink eyes filled with tears and she looked down at her lap. DS Gibbons waited patiently.

'He said to tell me that he was at peace now. No more pain. That he was so relieved to see that our son and daughter were supporting me and that he was still with me and loved me with all his heart.'

'That was a lovely message to receive,' DS Gibbons continued. 'Was this two days ago?'

'No, that was last week. She was most apologetic and said

she hoped she hadn't upset me. I have to say it was a bit of a shock, she walked me back home to make sure I was OK and said if I had any questions then she'd be happy to talk to me. I called her later that day and she agreed to come round and see if she could contact Tony for me.'

'And that visit took place?'

'Oh yes. She was very prompt. I haven't told anyone else about this you know, people wouldn't believe it, but she was a great comfort to me.'

'Had you arranged to see her again?'

'We talked about it, but hadn't set a date.'

'Do you mind me asking if she charged you for that visit?'

'She didn't charge me no, but I gave her some money. She was here several hours, you know, listening to me and sharing messages from my Tony. She doesn't have much money herself and had to get a train to get here so it was the least I could do.'

'So she intended to meet up again with you?'

Mrs Wilson nodded.

'Did she strike you as worried about anything?'

'No. Not at all. She was very relaxed, a lovely young woman.'

'I hope you don't mind me asking, but how much did you give to Ms Swift?'

'Why do you need to know that?'

DS Gibbons hesitated a moment, clearly looking for the right answer. 'It's useful for us to know how much cash she may have had with her. I presume it was cash?'

'Yes it was. Fifty pounds if you need to know. It was my choice to give it to her.' Mrs Wilson crossed her brows at DS Gibbons.

'Absolutely, Mrs Wilson.'

'I hope you find her and she's going to be alright.' Her face dropped into sadness again. 'She really is a lovely young woman and so talented.'

.   .   .

'If I didn't know better I'd start believing that Louise Swift really was a talented clairvoyant. Bumping into Mrs Wilson in the street and knowing all about her!' DS Gibbons said to Harrison as they returned to the station. 'Apart from the fact the train story was obviously not true.'

'I think she was good at targeting her clients and doing her research,' Harrison replied.

'Indeed. But maybe she targeted the wrong client. Old ladies seem to be her forte though.'

Back at the station, the staff and contents of the incident room had swelled since they'd last been there. All the desks and computers were in place, and all filled. Phones were ringing and it was a hive of activity.

DS Gibbons took one look at the room, said, 'I'm never going to be able to hold a briefing in here,' and disappeared back out again.

Harrison wandered over to some boards where information had been pinned up, scanning the contents for anything that he could use. A few minutes later, Gibbons returned, his ear stuck to his phone.

'That was Bones, he's officially confirmed it was Louise from dental records,' Gibbons conveyed to Harrison. 'Right, everyone, five minutes, finish up what you're doing and I want you all in the meeting room opposite this door for a briefing.'

The room erupted into another level of activity as officers grabbed whatever they needed for the briefing, or hastily ended what they were working on. Harrison strolled across to the meeting room, keen to find his favourite spot at the back of the room against the wall. There were more officers than there had been yesterday and the chairs quickly filled up.

Gibbons wasted no time in starting. The last couple of stragglers were just coming in as he began.

'We've had confirmation that the victim is Louise Swift, as we suspected. What I want now is some progress on finding her killers. Who wants to go first?'

A detective put her hand up. 'I've been checking the area for CCTV. Absolutely nothing. Nada. The entire village is a camera-free zone; the roads around Harmony House and the field where Louise was found are also all camera free. The nearest camera I can find is a traffic one on the road into town here, but unless the killers came from town, I can't see that's going to help us. I've asked for the footage anyway. I've also got footage from another camera on the other side of the village, but they're only going to be useful if the killers were outside a six-mile radius of that field.'

'Which doesn't rule out the village, Harmony House, or the Thistleford Community Church.'

'Correct, sir, and also there's a couple of farms and a small industrial estate within that area too.'

'Industrial estate? And they don't have cameras there?'

'No, sir.'

'Thanks, Nicky. OK, what about the house-to-house calls?'

'I led on that, sir,' a uniformed sergeant said from just in front of Harrison. 'We have now spoken to every person in that village. Not a single one of them heard or saw anything that night. Didn't even smell the smoke.'

'Including those whose homes are immediately adjacent to Louise's cottage?'

'Yup. On one side is an elderly lady who is clearly beginning to suffer from dementia. She's saying she didn't hear or see anything. On the other is a Jim Burrows, his wife, Laura, and young daughter. He works for Nick Rogers doing his garden and land maintenance. None of them heard anything. Laura Burrows says she was chatting to Louise that evening and everything was fine.'

'Is that possible? The killers may not have grabbed her from her home – she might have met them somewhere. But is it possible for that bonfire to have been created and lit with nobody in the village noticing?'

A sea of nonplussed faces looked back at DS Gibbons.

'I want to know the wind direction and weather conditions for that night. I want us to test to see if there are any points in the village, or surrounding area, where somebody can hear or see what's going on up in that field. Then I want the same tests done for Harmony House, the church group and any other residential dwellings. We have three communities living around that field. Three groups of people who could potentially be responsible or at least have heard something that evening and be witnesses. What we do have is a diary entry for the afternoon she was killed, which suggests that Louise had an appointment up at Harmony House. Did she never return? Did anybody see her go and come back?'

'Sir, her car is parked in the village.'

'She could have walked, it's a pleasant enough stroll and they don't let vehicles into their property. Or her car might have been brought back by one of the killers to avoid any suspicion. Get forensics combing every inch of it. Does it have satnav or a tracker?'

The officer who had mentioned the car nodded to say he'd get on it.

'And what about that bonfire?' Gibbons continued. 'Finn at Harmony House said the field was empty during the day. Now either he is lying, or that bonfire was created overnight. How long would it take to build a pile like that? I want all scenarios tested. We believe there were several people there so let's do the calculations and see if it's possible to create it in the dead of night without anybody noticing. How many people would it take? How was the wood transported there? Where was it stored?'

Heads nodded and notes were scribbled down.

'Anyone you spoke to offer any reasons as to why Louise would be targeted?' Gibbons addressed the uniformed sergeant again.

'Just that it could be somebody from her past or who she has been talking to online, but the Harmony House group and Community Church came up a fair bit. They don't seem to be very popular in the area. Convicted criminals was the main description of the Harmony House group, who seem to be the main suspects in the villagers' eyes.'

'And I take it still no sign of a computer or phone?'

'No. We found a charger for both at the cottage,' the female forensics officer who had spoken at the last team briefing said.

'Dr Lane and I went up to Harmony House and didn't exactly get a warm welcome. I want to talk to them but they're not going to cooperate unless we have a good reason to have a warrant and gain access. Are we still no closer to finding out about who they are?'

'The property is registered to the Harmony House collective and was bought by a Finn Smith five years ago. We have no records for any of the other residents.'

'So where did this Finn Smith find the kind of money to buy that place? Perhaps Louise Swift knew the answer to that question. How much have we found out about her background? Is there any possibility that she and Smith knew each other, or mixed in the same circles? I also want to know if the Harmony House group has any religious links. She was burnt as a witch; the graffiti in her cottage suggests that somebody or some group really believe that she held evil powers. We know there is a group of radical Christians in the area, the Thistleford Community church. Find out who they are and where they've come from. Any known issues? They could have been somewhere else before coming here and been forced to move on. And I want the backgrounds of every single person in the village checked. Who are these people? They're appearing to be good village folk. Are they? Should we definitely be looking at the ex-prisoners in the big house on the hill or the fundamental Christians who view witchcraft as evil?'

The room was silent, everyone thinking through the various possibilities and what they needed to do.

'OK, what you waiting for?' Gibbons said to them, eyebrows raised. They all got the message and headed out the room and back to their desks.

'We need to get into Harmony House,' Gibbons said to Harrison as the two of them followed the herd back across the corridor. 'They're obvious suspects, aren't they? A bunch of men with criminal convictions, although we don't have proof of that – we don't even know who they are because they're cut off from society, living some kind of feudal back-to-basics lifestyle. Plus, that diary entry... It's like a smoking gun.'

'They are obvious suspects, yes. But perhaps too convenient?'

'Yes, and no obvious motive, unlike the church group who are likely to view her gift, as Mark O'Neil called it, as evil. Either way, we've got no evidence against any of them, except a burnt body, so I can't go marching in there accusing them of murder.'

'I'll go to the Community Church group tonight and get a feel for them and their views, and I'll also focus on Louise Swift herself,' Harrison said to him. 'Have forensics finished at the cottage? I'd like to get back in there and take a good look around.'

'Sure. I'll double check for you, but probably not today, maybe in the morning.'

If Harrison couldn't get to know his victim better on her own turf, then he'd wind the clock back and see if he could find out more about her past life and how and why she ended up at

Thistleford. Ryan had told him that Louise hailed from their friend, Jack Salter's patch.

'DS Salter,' the familiar voice answered his phone call.

'Jack, it's me, Harrison.'

'Hi, mate? Why you ringing on my work phone?'

'Because it's a work call. I need your help with a case I'm on.'

'You need *my* help? Well that's a first. Not sure I'm any good at the funny business you tend to look at, but fire away.'

'We have a victim here, a Louise Swift, who I understand was last living in Lewisham before she moved here about two years ago. I need to get to know her better, talk to people who may have known her, and apparently she was pulled in for shoplifting by your colleagues. I wondered if you had any known associates listed for her, or if you or any of your team might know of any or have come across her?'

'Louise Swift,' Jack said aloud as he typed into his computer. There was silence for a moment, and then, 'Yeah, thought that name rang a bell. You called the right person. She was the girlfriend of Zack Elton. I put him away two years ago for burglary. She gave him an alibi but the jury didn't believe her. I couldn't get enough evidence to charge her with assisting him as they've both maintained his innocence. You say victim, is she dead?'

'Yes. I'm near Thistleford Village.'

'Shit, that's the witch case, isn't it? Might have known you'd be involved in that, but Louise, a witch? She did some new age stuff I seem to recall, but I'd never have imagined her on a broomstick with a cauldron. Didn't like cats either if I recall.'

'That is a storybook representation of a witch, Jack. In the religious context, people who don't worship the one true God or who claim to be mediums and speak to the dead and foresee the future, are as evil as those who cast spells.'

Harrison heard a chuckle from the other end of the phone. 'Ah, mate, you're so easy to wind up.'

Harrison humphed, he was used to being the butt of Jack's friendly jokes. 'Where's Zack Elton now, do you know?'

'Sure do. He's staying for the foreseeable at Belmarsh.'

'Don't suppose you and I could go and pay him a visit ASAP, do you? Is he likely to talk?'

'He might. We got on alright, one of those with a bit of respect for the law but just didn't want to abide by it. A bit old school. Depends what you want to know though, he was loyal to her, doted on her.'

'Just want to talk about her really, get to know what she was like.'

'Leave it with me and I'll see what I can do.'

Harrison knew that he could always rely on Jack Salter.

SIXTEEN

The Thistleford Community Church was on a small farm complex just outside of the village. A sign on the wall that ran along the road, proudly proclaimed: *God's Word is Your Salvation*. Harrison wondered if they would find his Harley Davidson fitted in with their idea of righteousness. As he rumbled into the yard, two people crossing to the barn that had a big white cross on its gable end, looked his way and hurried inside. A couple of smaller barns, which seemed to have also been converted into some kind of residential usage, sat along the outer edge of the yard.

Before Harrison had even taken his helmet off, the man he'd met along the lane near the field, came out to greet him.

'Welcome to our church, brother,' he said to him, smiling and arms open. 'I'm so pleased you have come along to share in our rejoicing of the Lord.'

As they walked towards the church, Harrison could see a welcome party forming in the entranceway.

'This is my wife, Bethany, who you met earlier, and sister Sarah.'

A timid young woman with long dark hair bobbed her head

at him and smiled coyly. Both women were wearing white lacy scarves over their hair. From their appearance and their mannerisms, Harrison could instantly see this was a patriarchal church where women were not given the same status as men, Nick Rogers had been right about that. Harrison wasn't sure if Sarah was a blood relative or just a member of the congregation.

'This here is brother Adam and brother Stephen.'

Two middle-aged men looked at Harrison warily.

'I can introduce you to the others after the service,' the man who had still yet to give Harrison his name, continued. 'Sarah will show you where to sit.'

The timid young woman stepped forward shyly and smiled at Harrison again, before turning and walking between the wooden pews to a couple of rows from the front.

The barn had been painted white inside, religious imagery and crucifixes attached to the bare wooden walls, while the pews and the pulpit in front looked as though they'd probably been bought second hand from another church.

Harrison had been into many churches, of all denominations – he'd visited Satanic ritual sites and witnessed some of the worst evil that came from the minds of people who validated their actions with a warped belief system that defied morality – but something about this seemingly innocuous church made the vagus nerve in his gut send fight or flight responses to his brain. He could feel his breathing speed up slightly and the blood flow to his muscles increase. Harrison tried to take deep breaths, to relax, but something had made him uneasy. Perhaps it was the similarity of the building and the familiar smell of damp wood, which reminded him of the barn in which his mother had been found, dead. Or maybe it was the atmosphere, a repressed extremism that threatened to overwhelm him if let loose.

He looked around to see Sarah smiling sweetly at him and was reminded of a movie he'd once seen at university, *The Step-*

ford Wives. Was Sarah really happy here, or did she feel down-trodden and exploited?

'You'll love Pastor Sam,' she whispered to him as though she was a schoolgirl telling a friend about a crush she had on a teacher.

The rest of the congregation sat patiently waiting for the service to start, talking in hushed reverent whispers. Was this a church led by fear or love? Harrison suspected the former.

A few minutes later and the lights suddenly went out, leaving just a few candles around the walls and at the front, where a raised wooden platform formed the sanctuary. The brightest light came from candles which flickered at the base of a large cross. Almost immediately the congregation around him fell totally silent.

The black tendril of fear that had entered Harrison's mind earlier that day, grew larger.

The doors of the barn were suddenly flung open, nearly making him jump. A blast of cool air fed down the congregation, flickering the candles and creating dancing shadows on the walls. Some flames blew out, bringing more darkness, but in its wake came a long white robed figure, arms and eyes raised to the large wooden cross at the front of the church.

He was a tall thin man with long hair and a beard. If you were casting an actor to play the role of Jesus in a film based on the popular depictions of him, then this man would fit the bill. He walked to the front, bowed before the cross and then turned to look at his audience.

'Praise the Lord.'

The congregation echoed his words, 'Praise the Lord,' in unison.

'I want to talk to you today about salvation. There are those who have turned their backs on our Lord and rejected his word. Not only that but they have followed false prophets and false gods, but you must never waver in your devotion to our Lord.

Who so ever believeth in him should not perish but have eternal life. That's right, brothers and sisters, *eternal life* will come to all of you as your just reward for following the word of the one true God.'

And so the sermon began, with Pastor Sam quoting a whole menu of sins which resulted in those who persistently practised them losing their souls to the devil. It was hate speech masquerading as a fire and brimstone Christianity, and the congregation were lapping it up, smug in the belief that they had their place in heaven's eternal kingdom guaranteed.

There was no room for tolerance and diversity in this church. It was ruled by fear and fanaticism. It wasn't the most extreme that Harrison had heard, but it was clear this man prescribed to the Old Testament God and not the gentler version in the New Testament. Among the threats of judgement and being sent to hell for transgressions, there was also the promise that God would show the way to those who listened to his word allowing them to come back into the fold and find forgiveness and be saved. Harrison suspected some of that messaging was aimed at him. A little bit of scaremongering with a dose of portraying the church as a guiding light in this modern world of unrest, fear, and moral turmoil. Without a doubt, Pastor Sam wouldn't have tolerated Louise Swift's alleged gifts of being a medium. The question was whether he was extreme enough to have done something about it?

Once the sermon was over, the man who'd invited him, who Harrison learned was called Paul, introduced him to Pastor Sam.

'Welcome.' He reached out and clasped both of Harrison's big hands. Although this man was physically weaker than him and his hands considerably smaller, his grasp sent a shiver through Harrison's body and he had to resist the urge to pull away. He found himself lost for words. 'We hope you'll join us for some refreshments,' the pastor said to him, smiling, and

Harrison's attention was taken by his bright blue eyes which seemed to search into his soul.

'I knew you'd love him,' Sarah whispered to him excitedly as they walked out of the barn church, taking his silence as awe for her leader.

The silence of the congregation was contrasted to the chatter and noise that greeted him in one of the smaller barns. It had been converted into a communal kitchen and eating space, giving it a religious summer camp feel. The women were rushing around cooking and setting out the table or looking after the children, while the men were stood around talking earnestly. Sarah fluttered around Harrison, ensuring he had everything he could possibly want. He was invited to join the men and stood listening to their conversations, but offering up little of his own. When Pastor Sam arrived, this time out of his robes, he was immediately the centre of attention. He went to sit down at the head of the table, which clearly the rest of the men had all been waiting for, because they took their seats straight afterwards, with the women only following once the men were seated.

Harrison was shown to the other end of the table where he was joined by Sarah and Bethany, with Paul the nearest man. It didn't escape Harrison's notice that when Sarah took a plate of food to the pastor, he placed his hand on her rear for a lot longer than Harrison would have found polite.

A prayer was said by Pastor Sam, once everyone had their food in front of them, and then eating began. Conversation over the meal was mostly quite tame; Sarah and Bethany gently tried to get information out of Harrison about his beliefs and why he was there. He skirted around most of the questions but once everyone had relaxed a little, he started to ask some of his own.

'Are you Pastor Sam's girlfriend?' he asked Sarah, trying to make his question as innocent sounding as possible. She looked at Bethany a little panicked, and both women gave a forced giggle.

'Pastor Sam doesn't have girlfriends. We are all his followers. We are here because of him.'

'But you are married to Paul?' Harrison asked Bethany.

'Yes. Paul is my legal husband.'

The answer was far more ambiguous than he'd have liked to hear, but he dropped the subject in case either woman took offence.

'Why were you up near that field where the witch was burnt?' he asked Sarah.

'We travel around looking for those who might need our Lord's salvation.' She smiled sweetly at him.

'So, what do you think about what happened?'

She stopped and studied his face for a moment. 'About the burning?'

He nodded.

'She was raised for the devil and carried out his work. God's judgement was meted out.'

'The devil's work?'

'Yes. She was a false prophet, claiming to speak with those who are departed. Only our Lord can do that. It is only his voice that she should have been listening to.'

'So what happened was her punishment?'

'Yes. Of course. The Bible is clear, anyone who practises witchcraft, or who is a medium or spiritist, is detestable to the Lord. It is forbidden.'

'Did you know her then?'

At this point Sarah got up. 'Excuse me,' she said and walked over to Pastor Sam.

Harrison suspected he'd been rumbled, but tried Bethany to see if she would still talk to him.

'Did you know her?' he asked. 'The woman who burnt?'

'I know only that her moral compass was broken. She had turned away from the Lord and was cavorting with the devil,' she replied, the sweet smile on her face not matching the words she spoke.

'So you did know her? How?' Harrison pushed. From the corner of his eye he could see that Sarah's conversation with the pastor was now over and he was talking to some of the other men.

Bethany shook her head and looked towards her husband and the other end of the table, her eyes afraid.

'Brother, you want to know about what happened in the field above the village?' Bethany's husband Paul leant over.

'I was just enquiring what you thought about what had taken place.'

'Why? Are you from the police? The media?' Paul asked. 'Are you here on false pretences?' His tone was no longer friendly, but hard and businesslike.

As Paul said this, Harrison saw that several of the other men, led by Pastor Sam, had risen from the table and were now approaching him.

'I was just interested,' Harrison said. 'You were there and I wondered if you'd known her.' But he knew it was time to go. He'd outstayed his welcome. As the men reached him, he stood up, drawing himself to full height.

'I think you should leave now. I don't think you are a genuine believer,' Pastor Sam addressed him. 'I think you are a serpent in our garden.'

Harrison held his hands up as though surrendering. 'My apologies, I didn't come here to cause trouble.'

'What did you come here for? Whatever it is, it isn't for salvation and the word of our Lord.'

'I'm going,' Harrison said, 'thank you for your hospitality.' He walked through the room with every pair of eyes boring into his back, but his own eyes weren't on them. They were on the photographs that lined the walls of the dining room area, and on one photograph in particular, in which he recognised a familiar face.

The men followed him outside, standing arms folded across their chests as they watched him get on his bike and ride away. It wasn't until halfway down the road that Harrison realised he was shaking slightly and it wasn't just from the adrenaline. He hadn't been afraid of the group of men, he'd taken on more fearsome fights than that. It was the steady gaze of Pastor Sam which had chilled him to his core.

Were these people capable of violence in the search for their salvation? It was clear they thought Louise had received God's punishment, the question was, had they meted it out, or merely supported its outcome? And did somebody in the village help them achieve that goal?

SEVENTEEN

Harrison had the worst night's sleep he'd experienced in well over a decade. His dreams were filled with the wrath of God and the scowling faces of those at the Thistleford Community Church. In his dreams they'd been angrier, more threatening, and at one point he'd even found himself tied to a cross as they approached with a burning torch to set him ablaze.

But it was in the morning that the worst experience came. He opened his eyes to see the face of Pastor Sam leering down at him, with his hands around his throat. Harrison felt like he couldn't breathe, but he was unable to move as though he'd been drugged with a paralysis poison, and neither could he make any sound. All he could do was watch as Pastor Sam squeezed his hands tighter around his throat. It seemed to go on forever, but in fact it was just split seconds before full consciousness returned to him and Pastor Sam disappeared from his hotel room. Harrison shot upright in the bed, his heart pounding, a sweat erupting all over him. It wasn't real, but it might as well have been for the effect it had on his mind and body.

It took him half an hour to calm down, using all his meditation and breathing techniques. Consciously slowing and deepening his breaths, focusing on every muscle to ensure they relaxed. He'd felt like sobbing, the shock and emotions that had hit him were overwhelming, but he knew what he'd just experienced. It was a hypnagogic hallucination coupled with sleep paralysis, he'd had a handful of similar incidents when he was a child and back then, before he understood what they were, they were even more terrifying.

They don't happen to everyone, but if they do it's in the period between sleep and wakefulness; when the brain and body are leaving REM sleep, but aren't fully conscious. The last time that Harrison suffered from them had been after he and his mother had left the UK to go to the United States. Back then, he was just seven years old and had experienced several traumatic events, including the murder of one of their friends in a Satanic ritual in Nunhead Cemetery.

Going to Thistleford Community Church last night had woken some of the buried memories. Pastor Sam had reminded him of Desmond Manning, the head of the commune in which he and his mother had lived. They might be on opposite sides of the religious divide, Desmond worshipped Satan rather than God, but their tactics of fear and control were the same. Manning was now in prison and his evil wife was dead, but Harrison could easily imagine Pastor Sam whipping his congregation into a frenzy over Louise Swift and her sinful ways; stoning and burning her in the name of God.

In their eyes, they were surrounded by evil, modern society an anathema to the Old Testament's teachings, carrying out God's work wasn't a crime; it was the right thing to do, which would mean they wouldn't have viewed her death as a murder.

Harrison took a shower to try to wash the memory of his nightmares from his mind, but it only served to cleanse the sweat from his skin. When he'd finished, there was a text from Ryan on his phone.

Yo boss, you OK?

Fine. Why?

You seemed a little rattled last night. I'm looking
into the Community Church now. Will get some
info across to you ASAP.

Harrison sighed. Ryan was right. He had been rattled. The critical point was that while his visit had made clear that the Community Church was an extremist group of sorts, perhaps even a cult, he was no closer to proving who had murdered Louise Swift. He might have been rattled by his visit, but he could be sure that they were now going to be even more wary and that meant their job of finding evidence was going to be harder. What he needed was to get closer to Louise herself. Find out what motivated her in the work she did and whether she had any links with the Community Church.

Over breakfast, Harrison's prayers were answered when Jack's name came up on his phone. An hour later, Harrison was on his bike, heading to London and Belmarsh prison. Jack had pulled in a favour and got the go-ahead for a visit in super-quick time, the minute that Zack Elton had agreed it.

The journey down was a smooth one, the threatening clouds held back their rain, and he'd been able to check out of the hotel, pack his one little bag, and get down there in plenty of time. He'd contemplated going there and back in a day, but the temptation to stay in London at his own place had been too strong. He craved some familiarity and security, and his sanctuary was his apartment. He called DS Gibbons, filling him in on where he was going, and told him he'd be back tomorrow.

He and Jack had arranged to meet at a café so that they could arrive at the prison together. As he walked in, Harrison scanned the tables and quickly spotted the blond head and broad shoulders of his friend.

'Good to see you,' Jack said standing up to greet him and slapping him on the back. He was probably the only man who would feel brave enough to do that to Harrison, and it was only because they were such good friends.

'How's Marie doing?' Harrison asked after Jack's wife.

'Blooming is the only way to describe her,' Jack beamed back at him. 'She's so much better with this pregnancy. We're thinking it's going to be a girl. You know you hear that sometimes mothers are better at carrying one gender or the other.'

Harrison smiled, imagining his friends with a little girl to add to their family.

'You and Tanya should come over again soon, before we're knee-deep in nappies.'

'That would be good.' A smile of understanding passed between them. When Harrison had first started working with Jack, his wife Marie had been suffering from postnatal depression with their firstborn. It had been a tough time for them both and Harrison had been able to use his psychological training to suggest ideas that would help Marie to recover at a time when she was refusing help from anyone.

They were forever grateful to him but Jack had been fearful for Marie that having another child might bring it on again. Harrison had talked to them both, and Marie had spoken to her doctor. This time they were prepared in case it happened again, and they'd been totally honest with family and friends so that Marie wouldn't isolate herself like she had the first time. Jack was also ready to take some extra time off work to help. They were understandably apprehensive, but Marie's pregnancy had been a lot easier this time around and so there was a good chance she wouldn't fall victim to the depression so badly as before.

Harrison bought Jack another coffee and got himself a herbal tea before sitting down in front of his friend.

'Right, so, Zack Elton,' Jack began. 'Burglar and also a con artist, would take any opportunity to earn a bit of cash. Pretty successful at his work. Had himself a nice house and car and I think he's hidden some of it, but we were never able to trace anything more. He and Louise were together about three years before we arrested him. I don't think she was up to anything illegal before they became an item, but she had other talents. She was really smart. Could size up a person in a flash and talk her way out of Alcatraz. Like I said on the phone, we could never pin anything on her and so she walked and Zack wouldn't say a word against her.'

'Any ideas if they stayed in contact?'

'I don't know, but that would be handy for you if they did.'

'He may not have been told about her death yet, so we need to bear that in mind. She's only just been officially identified through dental records.'

'True, he won't be an official next of kin. We'll need to let the prison know then. It might hit him hard.'

It took them forty-five minutes to go through the security procedures at Belmarsh and sit down in the room where Zack Elton was going to meet them. When he came in, he let rip a big smile at the sight of Jack.

'DS Jack Salter, what a lovely surprise. To what do I owe this honour? Not trying to track down more of my ill-gotten gains, are you? I told you, there's nothing left.'

He was what someone might call a cheeky chappy, one of those characters who seemed to be forever smiling and at ease with himself. Clearly none the worse for being incarcerated.

'Zack, this is Dr Harrison Lane. He's a ritualistic crime psychologist, and wants to ask you a few questions.'

'Ooh err, I've never taken part in any rituals, what do you want with me? I only pray to the god of money.' Zack laughed at his own joke.

'Mr Elton,' Harrison began, 'before I start we need to give you some news which may be upsetting.'

Zack's face instantly fell solemn, his eyes searching the two faces in front of him for some clue as to what might be coming next.

'I'm very sorry to have to tell you, that your former girl-friend, Louise Swift, has been found murdered.'

A choking sound came from Zack and he clasped at his stomach. 'Louise? You sure?' he asked in a hoarse whisper, looking to Jack for confirmation.

'I'm afraid so, Zack,' Jack said gently.

'We were going to be together after I got out. She were waiting for me...' His voice choked off and his face had turned grey.

'Do you want us to give you a few minutes?' Jack asked.

Harrison let Jack take the lead, knowing that he and Zack had a prior relationship.

'Just a moment,' Zack said, swiping at his eyes with the back of his hand and giving a shuddering breath. 'You said murdered. Why? Who did it?' This time he looked to Harrison, a renewed energy in his voice.

'I'm part of the team investigating her death,' Harrison explained. 'I'm sorry but it wasn't pleasant. She was burnt on a cross as if she was a witch, just outside of the village of Thistleford.'

'Burnt!' Zack swore and jumped up from the chair he was sitting in, pacing up and down in front of them. 'Why? Why would anyone do that to her?'

'That's what I'm trying to understand and to do that I wanted to get to know her better and wondered if perhaps you could help.'

'Ask me anything. I want them to pay.' A steely determina-tion was in his eyes now and he sat back down, putting both elbows on the table and leaning in to Jack and Harrison.

'Why was she in Thistleford? Seems an odd choice after London,' he asked.

'She'd annoyed someone in Lewisham, someone you don't want to annoy. Know what I mean? She only did it to help me but it backfired on her. So, she moved away for a bit, somewhere quiet where she could keep her head down.'

'This someone, are they likely to have carried the grudge and killed her?'

'Nah. It weren't that bad and that certainly ain't their style. She just figured something out that she shouldn't have known, but they'll know she never told no one about it. No it weren't them. They've cooled down by now. But she was too smart for her own good sometimes. Maybe she found out stuff she shouldn't have about someone there.'

'Apart from her medium work, did she practise any kind of Wicca or witchcraft?'

Zack swore. 'No way, that wasn't her thing. She did crystals and stuff but that's so she could sell 'em to the punters. People like all that shit.'

'Do you have any idea why someone would accuse her of witchcraft?'

Zack shook his head sadly. 'One of them fundamental religious types maybe?'

'Did you speak to her?'

'Yeah, we talked on the phone and she wrote me too.'

'She wrote you letters?'

Zack nodded.

'Did she ever say she was worried about anybody or frightened?'

'No. She was doing alright. She had everything under control from what I could tell.'

'Did she talk about her life in the village?'

He nodded again.

'Would it be possible to see those letters?'

Zack looked down at his lap, thinking.

'Perhaps if we just asked the prison if we could copy them so that you weren't left without them?' Harrison added.

'Yeah, that would be OK.' Zack looked up at him. 'I want them caught, so if you think it will help.'

'Did she like the villagers?' Harrison asked now.

Zack shrugged.

'What about the Thistleford Community Church, was she ever involved with that at all, or did she have any problems with it?'

Zack frowned and thought. 'I think she had someone shouting abuse at her once, a religious nutter she called 'em. At one of them spiritualist fairs, you know. They were there with signs telling everyone they were going to go to hell. Not sure if it was that lot or not.'

'And did she ever mention a place called Harmony House?'

'Rings a bell, yeah. She said she'd seen someone from the past who lived nearby. An old mate of her dad's.'

'Do I read that to mean an ex con?' Harrison asked.

'Yeah. Her old man was never around when she was growing up. She certainly didn't get her brains from him. As soon as he got out, he'd go and get caught again. I think he got life the last time. Don't reckon he had any friends except those he'd made inside.'

'So she saw someone she recognised; did she say if she spoke to him at all?'

Zack shrugged and shook his head.

'And do you know if she was blackmailing anyone? It doesn't matter to her now if she was, so you won't be betraying her, but it could be a motive for her murder.'

'Listen, I talk to her on a prison phone and get letters which are read by the screws. Do you really think she'd tell me something like that?'

By the time they'd been talking for an hour, Zack looked

emotionally exhausted, the shock of hearing about Louise's death was starting to sink in. Harrison felt he'd got enough information and that Zack needed a break.

'Make sure you get 'em,' Zack said to him as he left to go back to his cell with the prison officer. 'You wanna know anything else, you know where I am.'

Harrison and Jack went straight to the warden's office to let them know that Zack had received bad news and might need some support. They also requested that an officer fetched the letters from him so they could be copied. That took another hour or so, and then the process of copying them and making sure everything was signed off and authorised, a further forty-five minutes.

By the time they left it was almost rush hour for the end of the working day and so Jack decided to head home to his family.

'Thanks for your time, Jack,' Harrison said as they finally left the prison.

'It's alright, mate, Sandra gave me the green light. You know she always has a soft spot for you.'

Harrison smiled, remembering Jack's boss, Detective Superintendent Sandra Barker. He had a great deal of respect for her and was forever grateful that she'd had faith in his Ritualistic Crime unit when he'd first started it at the Met. 'Thank her for me, would you?'

'I will. And don't forget, you and Tanya only have about three more weeks before we go into imminent birth lockdown and then full-on new baby mode.'

'I'll not forget. I'm going to head back to Thistleford in the morning to see if this new information can get me any closer to understanding who killed Louise.'

'If I know you, you'll be back by the evening,' Jack joked.

'See you soon, mate,' Harrison said. He was keen to get back to his own flat. Focusing on Zack and Louise had given him a welcome break from the way he'd felt that morning, but he wanted to start reading the batch of around thirty letters he was holding that had been sent by Louise Swift. He hoped they'd help him get inside her head and understand her relationships with the villagers and those at Harmony House and the Community Church. There was still the chance that it was someone from the town or surrounding area, but Harrison didn't think so. Whoever built that bonfire knew exactly where to find the materials they needed and how to do it without anyone else noticing. That meant it had to be someone very local.

EIGHTEEN

Before he got on his bike to head to London Docklands and his flat, Harrison texted Tanya. He hadn't been sure if he was in the right frame of mind for company, but he felt bad if he was in town and didn't get in contact. They saw each other so infrequently as it was, thanks to his travelling for work.

> Don't suppose you're around tonight and fancy a takeaway in the Docklands do you?

She replied straight away.

> You're back already! Thought you'd be gone a while. I can be round about half seven.

> Got to head back in the morning, but be great to see you.

Harrison wasn't the kind of man to use emojis and x to denote kisses, but he got a smiley face and a big X back from Tanya.

As soon as Harrison got into his flat, he realised that he needed to release the tension of last night. He craved the mind-numbing effort of strenuous physical exercise. He threw his bag down and got changed into his running gear and went straight back out again. He still had nearly two hours before Tanya would be here and he wanted to read Louise's letters to Zack, which gave him just enough spare time for exercise and a shower.

Harrison headed for the riverside where he knew he could get a straight stretch to run. He started steadily, his muscles feeling tight and tense, warming up the big quadriceps in his thighs until he could feel them elastic and supple, wanting more. Gradually he built up his speed, his biceps pumping back and forth, pushing him on, his big chest starting to expand and contract with the breaths which grew deeper and faster. Every muscle started to do its work, the tight band of abdominal muscles around his middle helping to squeeze the breath from his lungs so they could fill again with oxygen.

As he ran he thought about Louise Swift and the tiny village where horror had built a bonfire. She was no angel, but she was also no witch. The villagers said they universally loved her, and the Community Church, while condemning what she did, professed that they weren't violent, so could Harmony House hold the key? Zack said that Louise had made contact with someone from her dad's past, an ex con. Were those gates and walls protecting a cult of seasoned criminals, men who would stop at nothing to protect their current lifestyle? It was possible, but Harrison couldn't get away from the feeling he'd got the moment he walked into the Community Church. Everything fitted, the religious motivation, their hatred of those who didn't follow their interpretation of the Bible.

Harrison ran on, his breathing becoming more laboured and his skin starting to feel moist with sweat. He ran until he could feel his muscles starting to tire and then he turned back round and headed for home. This was where the pain kicked in, the discipline, the determination to keep on pushing until he reached his flat. As his lungs and muscles started to burn with the exertion, his mind went back to Louise Swift and the terror that must have gone through her mind as the smoke from the fire entered her lungs and the flames reached her legs. How could anyone watch that torture and then act as if nothing had happened the next day? To do that took a psychopathic personality, extreme hatred, or perhaps the justification of knowing you were doing the Lord's work for him and your reward would be heaven. Any one of the groups of people around Thistleford could have done it.

As he neared home, the pain in his taut muscles dominated his whole mind and body. He could think of nothing else but getting to the refurbished Dockland warehouse that contained his apartment, and letting his body catch up with the oxygen it craved.

He did it, stopping in front on a patch of grass, bending over double and leaning on his thighs while he caught his breath. As he did so he began to stretch, expelling the lactic acid that wanted to build up in his muscles and leave them sore. He would do some more stretches indoors, away from the potentially cold breeze, to maintain flexibility.

Once he had stretched his muscles, Harrison stripped off his running gear and took a shower. He let the hot water clean him and soothe his body, before ending with a blast of cold. By the time he'd redressed and drunk a glass of water, he still had enough time to refill his glass and go and sit on the sofa with the letters from Zack. Harrison knew that Louise would have been mindful of the letters being read by the authorities, but perhaps there'd be a clue in there somewhere as to who may have murdered her.

It felt like prying, reading the personal messages to someone that Louise clearly did love. From the way she talked, it seemed that Zack had been telling the truth: she was biding her time somewhere quiet while she waited for him to do his time.

Harrison wondered how Zack was faring after they'd dropped the bombshell news on him. As they weren't married or next of kin, he wouldn't have been officially told, but Harrison hoped that the prison gave him some support. He couldn't imagine how difficult it must be to be locked away where you could do nothing to help the person you loved.

Tanya was the reason that Harrison had pressed pause in the hunt for his own mother's killer. After her life had been threatened and he'd realised how well connected the killer was, Harrison had felt the risk was far greater than he was prepared to wager. Those who he had spoken to about what had happened, had also been warned off. He wasn't going to give up, but he knew he had to be smarter in how he investigated.

Harrison thought about the postcard that he kept in a box in his bedroom. His mother had sent it to a friend, his university professor who had mentored Harrison through the difficult years after her death. He knew it was a clue, a message she'd sent when she knew that her life might be in danger. He also knew the place that was on the postcard. He could see it right now, the country road that ran through the Welsh countryside, mountains in the background, and the site where they'd lived on the run-down farm, just a few hundred yards along. Harrison had been convinced that his mother had left him some evidence or something that would enable him to catch her killer.

Last month he'd travelled down there, fighting back the apprehension in his gut as he'd approached the place that held so many bad memories for him. He'd insisted on going alone – just in case he found more than he'd expected. In the event, he'd found nothing. He'd looked in the little place behind some stones where his mother used to leave him secret messages, pretending to be from the Welsh dragon that lived in the hills. She would hide them there before she went to work because she knew he'd go and meet her off the bus when she came back. Every time he would look for his letter and then sit and wait for her so he could tell her what the dragon had said. The memory brought back a smile to his lips.

He'd even gone back to the old farm. It wasn't much more now than a pile of stones and rotting wood. There was nothing but the wind to greet him and the ghosts of those who had haunted his childhood days. He'd searched for hours, wracking his brains for the hidden meaning in the postcard. There had to be something he was missing. You didn't send a postcard with no other writing on it to a friend, for no reason.

Eventually, he'd had to accept that there was nothing there that he could find, at least not that time. He'd returned to London feeling defeated and angry at himself. He'd been so sure that he was going to make a breakthrough. What he realised was that time had made him lose the connection to whatever message the postcard held. So much had passed since then, memories corrupted, theories imagined, that he couldn't be sure of what his mother had meant.

Harrison finished his glass of water and sat still for a few moments, enjoying the feeling of his blood pumping around his system, imagining it powering up his brain with the oxygen it carried. Then, he turned his concentration to Louise Swift's letters. These were from the here and now, her voice from the grave that was loud and clear. He needed to listen to that voice and find her killers.

NINETEEN

Harrison's impromptu takeaway dinner with Tanya and their evening together had started off as a welcome respite from the situation back at Thistleford, but it didn't quite go as he'd planned. While they waited for their dinner delivery, they'd sat on the sofa, catching up on each other's week. Harrison told her about his sleep paralysis and hallucination.

'Maybe you should get some counselling, what happened to you as a child is still affecting you,' she said.

'It's bound to affect me. Childhood trauma stays with you, it moulds you into the kind of adult you are. I'll be fine,' he said dismissively.

There was silence as the two of them stared out the big window and watched the River Thames as it flowed past.

'It would be nice to be watching a movie with you, have you thought about getting a TV?' Tanya asked.

'I watch the TV when I'm at yours and most of it is rubbish. Why would anyone want to watch a fake reality TV show about dating that is just like every other fake reality TV show and features contestants that all look the same. I don't get it.'

'You don't have to watch *Love Island*, there's plenty of other good stuff on.'

Harrison hmphed, not convinced.

Some bats shot across their eyeline in the window, chasing insects on the wing.

'Did you know that bats were around in the dinosaur days, and that a quarter of all mammals are bats? They're a pretty successful species,' Tanya said to him, trying to lighten the atmosphere. 'I watched a documentary on them a couple of weeks back.'

'They get a mixed reaction from people, depending on the culture. The Chinese think they bring good luck and happiness, but in Nigeria they're thought of as witches, and of course in Europe we have the more recent vampire connotations,' Harrison said to her, ever the information junkie.

'I quite like them,' Tanya replied. 'Although I'm sure Jack would be making a joke at this point about me being batty or something equally as silly.'

'I saw Jack today and he invited us over for dinner, said we should book a date before they're consumed by the new baby,' Harrison said to her, stroking her head.

'That will be nice, but I don't mind babies. I'd be happy to babysit for them when they're ready too. Be good practice for when I have my own.' Tanya smiled up at him.

Harrison's face must have given away the horror that had suddenly gripped him.

'Don't panic, I'm not pregnant.' She giggled. 'I just mean one day. You know, I'd love to be a mother.' Tanya stayed watching him and then sat up to get a better look at his face. 'Don't you want to be a father? I mean, not now but, you know, sometime in the future?'

'It's not something I've given any thought to,' he replied honestly. 'I never had a father and so I don't think I'd know how.'

'You would. You'd make a great dad.'

Harrison must have still not looked convinced because Tanya dropped the subject and they sat in silence for a few moments.

'My landlord came round yesterday. Said she has split up from her boyfriend and she wants to move back into the flat. I've got two months to find a new place.'

'That's a shame, you liked it there.'

'Yes, and the rent was reasonable. I've been looking and I'm going to have to move out further to get comparable rent.'

'Why don't you share with Rachel? She's got a two-bedroom flat and you two get on really well.'

Tanya sighed and turned again to look at him.

'Yeah I guess, not sure she wants me there permanently though.'

'Ask her. And let me know when you need to move, and I'll help you with your stuff.'

It was at that point the front doorbell rang so Harrison got up to go and get their food. When he returned, Tanya had disappeared off to the toilet.

She came out of his room where she'd obviously been to the en suite. 'Where's the new wardrobe then?' she asked, her brow furrowed.

'In the spare room. I don't need it in my room because there's enough space for my clothes; it makes more sense to put it in the spare room for visitors.'

Tanya didn't reply and for a moment Harrison thought she'd gone to take a look, but she was standing there, silently watching him as he got plates and cutlery out for their dinner.

'Is that what I am, a visitor?' she asked.

Harrison stopped and looked at her, confused as to her meaning.

'Do you only want me to be a *visitor*?' Tanya asked.

'You're my only visitor, Tanya, apart from Ryan. I don't have time for one thing.'

'No. You don't.'

'Come and sit down before it all goes cold. Do you want a water?'

Tanya sat down and they ate their food in silence.

'Is it OK?' Harrison asked, concerned that she didn't like the food or wasn't feeling well. He couldn't believe that where he'd put the wardrobe could possibly have upset her.

'It's fine.'

Harrison was hungry and so carried on eating. Tanya seemed to be just pushing her food around.

'What's wrong?' Harrison finally asked again.

Tanya put her knife and fork down and paused a moment as she thought. Harrison put his cutlery down too in order to concentrate on what she was about to say. She was clearly upset about something.

'I'm not...' She sighed and took a deep breath. 'I don't want to put any pressure on you. About us. But I'm not sure where we are heading.'

'I thought we were fine.'

'We are, but...'

'I did say that I was going to have to be away a lot. You know how important my work is to me.'

'Yes I know. Look, I think we're both tired. You've had a stressful couple of days, and I've been really busy at work too. I'm going to head home and let you get a good night's sleep. You're up early again.' Tanya stood and looked around for her bag and jacket.

'You haven't finished your food,' Harrison said to her.

'I've had plenty, thank you.' She kissed him and then turned and started to walk towards the front door.

Harrison didn't know whether he should go after her, ask her to stay, or what? In the end, he said, 'Goodnight, let me know you're home safely and I'll see you when this case is finished.'

She turned and gave a weak smile. 'Sure. Goodnight.'

Afterwards, while he'd waited for her to text to say she was home, he'd thought about what had been said. She wanted more commitment from him, but he really wasn't sure that he was ready to do that just yet. Was he being unfair to her? He had so many things on his mind, and his reaction to the Thistleford Community Church had taken him by surprise, pulling the rug out from under his feet. He'd thought he was on top of those emotions, but the last twenty-four hours showed they were merely hibernating under the surface. How could he be a good long-term partner, let alone a father, when he was still consumed by the need to find his mother's killer?

His run and the previous night's poor sleep did at least help him to drift off quickly. But there were still vivid nightmares which now included a traumatised Tanya, who he couldn't protect.

He didn't exactly feel refreshed in the morning, but nevertheless, with the information he'd gleaned from Zack and Louise's letters, Harrison shot back up the motorway and to the town police station where he'd arranged to meet DS Gibbons for a debrief.

They were rendezvousing in a café on the high street and when Harrison arrived, Gibbons was already at a table, a mug of coffee in front of him. He looked up from his phone when Harrison's tall shadow fell over the table.

'Morning, thought we might get more peace in here to talk, that cramped office is doing my head in. Can't be doing with the noise. I'll get you a drink, what's your poison?'

'Don't worry, I'll get it, I'm up.' Harrison replied. 'Want anything to eat?' he added. Takeaways had that bizarre effect on him. Filled him up when he ate them and then made him feel extra hungry the next morning. Probably an indication of the amount of sugar that was in them. Harrison made a promise to himself to eat healthily tonight to make up for it. Eating healthily right now in the café gave him limited options. He opted for two pots of porridge – one would definitely not touch the sides – a chamomile tea, and a cheese croissant for Gibbons.

'So, shall I go first?' Gibbons said to him as he sat down. 'Thanks for letting us know about that photograph of Charley Jones at the Community Church. While you were gone, I went round to her house, but her mother said she wasn't in and had gone to a friend's. I've tried her mobile but there's been no reply. Mrs Jones said that Charley had started going to the church after her GCSE exams. *She was searching for some meaning in her life*, was what she said. Didn't find it though she reckons. Left after a few months.'

'Charley has a key to Louise's cottage. She could have let someone in.'

'I know. So you think that this Pastor Sam and his congregation are extremists who could be capable of a murder like this?'

'I've met people like Pastor Sam before. They're charismatic and persuasive. Once he has people under his spell, they'll do whatever he asks.'

'Well, we've still got nothing that gives us an opportunity to go in there with a warrant.'

'What about Charley? They could have kidnapped her, fearful that she'll spill the beans, or maybe she's hiding out there and they're protecting her.'

'There's nothing to suggest that she's in any danger. I'll keep trying her mobile and go back to her house, see if I can track her down.'

Harrison nodded, but he was still extremely concerned about Charley's welfare.

'We've been going through Louise Swift's bank account,

and that's not counting anything she may have got in cash. It was very healthy. She certainly wasn't strapped for cash as she'd told Rogers or Violet, there was around £23,000 in the current account and we're trying to find out if she had any others. We know she got around £10,000 out of Violet over the last eighteen months, and we'd already seen that the rent payments to Rogers stopped, but we couldn't see any payments from him coming the other way. There were, however, lots of other deposits made electronically from various people, some of them the villagers, some of them people we don't know. I'm presuming these were all her clients because amounts varied from £60 to £400.'

'Did you find any cash in her cottage?'

'No. And we can be sure she took a fair few payments in cash so that offers up a robbery aspect to the motive too.'

'Have we asked the villagers if they paid her in cash or electronically?'

'We know that some of them paid cash. She preferred it apparently – and not surprisingly as she didn't want the tax man after her. We couldn't find any financial links between her and Harmony House, or the Community Church.'

'That's not surprising though, is it? Harmony House don't have electricity or modern technology, according to Finn, so that's going to mean they only deal in cash, and I hardly think the church is going to be where she'd find friends.'

'Yup, exactly. For the Harmony House lot, off grid means out of sight of the authorities. What we'd really like to know is the state of their bank balance, but without a good reason to look, we're scuppered. What we did find out is that Finn is an ex con. Rogers was right about that. He was sent down for aggravated burglary and manslaughter, which raises some interesting questions.'

'Mmhm, well, Zack Elton was still her boyfriend – Louise was writing to him. He's just over two years into serving his seven-year term at Belmarsh and they were going to get together again when he got out. He didn't think there was anyone from her past who would be likely to do this to her, but he gave us around thirty letters she'd sent to him. Most of its personal stuff, but she does talk about the villagers and mentions that she bumped into and recognised a man who used to be in prison with her dad. Said his name was Maggot and he lived at Harmony House.'

'So she did have a link with that place, interesting.'

'Yes and her letters showed how astute she was with people, she found everyone's weak spots, what drove them and what made them insecure, and she said, "Think I might be saving myself a bit of money and going rent free." But she didn't go into any details, obviously because anything illegal would be picked up by the prison authorities.'

'So she may have been blackmailing Rogers?'

'It's certainly a possibility, but she could also have been blackmailing others and if she had that appointment at Harmony House on the day she died, then that may have been to go and see this Maggot person.'

'Perhaps that's where Finn got his money from to buy that place. Blackmail, robberies, etc. I'll get the financial crime team to dig around and trace where it came from.'

Harrison was about to say something else when Gibbons's mobile phone rang.

He sighed. 'Thought it had been too quiet, let me just take this, it's the incident room.'

'Sir. Just had a call in from one of the team up at the field.' Harrison could hear the faint voice on the other end of the line; they sounded slightly breathless, he could tell that meant either anxious or excited. 'Someone from Harmony House has just turned up at the field and said he wants to report a murder.'

TWENTY

When Harrison and DS Gibbons arrived at the gates to Harmony House, there were already two squad cars and a forensics van parked up in the semi-circle of gravel outside.

'What's going on? Why aren't they letting anyone in?' DS Gibbons jumped out the car, slamming the door in his wake. By the time Harrison had joined him at the gate entrance, a heated discussion was underway. Gibbons was talking to a different man to the one they'd seen last time they were there, but he too sported a beard and hair that was down to his shoulders, pulled back in a ponytail.

'You can't bring those vehicles in here. I've told them they can come in, but on foot. We don't allow vehicles on our land.'

'But we've got equipment to carry,' a forensic officer looked to Gibbons.

'You know that we have the right to enter as a murder has taken place here,' DS Gibbons said calmly to the man behind the gate. 'I appreciate your wishes but we need to come in immediately to assess the crime scene before any evidence deteriorates.'

'We moved him into the chapel, he's alright in there.'

'You moved the body?' DS Gibbons's tone of voice raised an octave. Harrison wondered how long he was going to keep his cool.

'Yes. We thought it would be cooler in the chapel while we decided what to do.'

'Decided what to do? Did you not call straight away? What time was he killed?'

'We found him this morning, about six thirty.'

'Why didn't you call us straight away?'

'We don't have a phone, and we had to discuss what to do.'

DS Gibbons took a deep breath. 'OK, we need to come in immediately, are you going to open these gates or do we have to force our way in?'

'Keep your bloody hair on, I said you can come in, just no cars.'

'Fine. No cars.'

'I can help you carry some stuff.' Harrison turned to the forensics officer who looked like he was about to burst into tears.

'Thank you,' he said, his shoulders visibly dropping with relief. 'I just don't know what's with these people. I told him the van's electric anyway.'

While Harrison waited at the back of the forensics van, he spotted a box of white protective suits.

'You don't happen to have an XX large size in those, do you?' he said, remembering the uncomfortable hour he'd spent in DS Gibbons's under-size suit.

'Sure, help yourself,' the grateful officer replied. 'Can you manage these two boxes for me?' he asked, presenting Harrison with two plastic boxes full of various chemicals and testing equipment. 'I've no idea what we're going to find in there, but I want to ensure we don't lose any more time and evidence.'

Seven of them gathered outside the gate, DS Gibbons,

Harrison, two forensic officers and three uniformed police officers. The man behind the gate gave them all a final once-over like some border control officer, as though they could have somehow secreted a vehicle in their midst, and at last undid the huge lock that secured the gates.

They filed in and then waited while he locked the gates again.

'This way,' he said to them.

'We need to look at where you found the body,' DS Gibbons explained to him.

'I didn't find it.'

'Where it was found then, by whoever found him.'

'That was Maggot. He's still with him I think. Devastated he is. We all are.'

Harrison and Gibbons exchanged a glance when they heard the name.

They had walked through the wooden structure which turned out to consist of an empty room apart from some comfy chairs, a table and a wood-burning stove. Little more than a wooden barn. In front of them was a long gravelled driveway that swept around a corner.

'How far is it?' Gibbons asked, attempting to hide the frustration in his voice and not totally succeeding.

'The chapel's round the corner. It's further to the house,' the man replied.

'So, was Finn very religious? Are you all men of faith?' Gibbons fished. Harrison knew what he was digging for.

'No. Not Finn. There's a couple of us who believe. I'm not one of them. I told you we put him in the chapel because it seemed better than leaving him out in the sun.'

'What do they call you?' Harrison asked the man, reducing his own stride to fall into step with him.

'Cooper.'

'How do you transport things around here then, Cooper?' Harrison asked.

'We have hand carts and wheelbarrows.'

'Where would we find one of those handcarts, it would be useful for carrying equipment?'

'There's one at the chapel. We used it to take Finn there.'

Harrison heard a groan from the forensics officer behind him. They wouldn't be able to use that cart: it would now be considered part of the evidence.

'How long have you been here?' Harrison asked.

'I'm one of the more recent ones,' Cooper said, 'came here about a year ago.'

'Where are you from?' Gibbons asked him.

'Don't matter where I'm from, just that I'm here.'

Gibbons threw Harrison another look. He'd already spotted the tattoo on the man's arm which suggested he'd been in prison.

'So how does this place work then? Do you all have certain jobs or muck in together?' Harrison picked the conversation back up.

'Bit of both. If you're good at something then you tend to do it, but we all have to do some stuff like collecting firewood, security, cleaning, and farming.'

'Security?'

'Yeah, looking after the gate.'

'What do you like doing?'

The man smiled for the first time. 'I like growing the food. It's good working in the field, planting something, watching it grow and then knowing we can eat it. I don't mind a bit of cooking too but that's Paxo's territory mostly.'

'How did you hear about this place?'

'Through a mate.'

'When did you last see Finn alive?'

'Last night. We had a few jars. Make our own home brew, you know. Sat around the fire pit for a bit.'

'How did he seem? His usual self?'

'Mmmh, bit quieter I'd say. Yeah, didn't say much at all come to think of it.'

'Did he go out at all yesterday? Leave the grounds?'

'I dunno. I was in the field all day. You'll have to ask whoever was on gate duty. It's all very chilled here, we don't keep tabs on each other, you know. Here we are.'

They'd rounded the bend and to the right was a small stone chapel, outside of which sat a wooden hand cart. What captured everyone's attention, however, was the sweeping gravel driveway up to the main house. What would have once been manicured lawns and gardens, was now an agricultural smallholding. On the left-hand side, various crops were growing like a giant allotment. On the right, were livestock. Harrison could see a couple of cows, some sheep, pigs, and chickens. The whole scene looked incongruous in front of the splendour of the large stone mansion which had a gothic look to its architecture.

'Wow!' was all Gibbons said.

'Good, aint it,' Cooper replied.

Harrison wasn't sure that Gibbons's exclamation had been an expression of how impressed he was, but he didn't say anything further.

'Where is everyone?' Harrison asked Cooper.

'Some are inside the chapel, some in the house, but none of us have felt much like working.'

'Is everyone here? I mean has anybody left?' Gibbons asked.

'No. We're all here. Nobody has anything to hide.' Harrison detected defensiveness in Cooper's tone.

'What's going to happen to this place? Finn owned it, didn't he?' Harrison changed the subject.

'He bought it, but he told us it belongs to all of us. There's like some kind of company or trust or something that means it has to stay as it is for us to use. No one can sell it and chuck us out.'

The group reached the entrance to the chapel and moved through the doorway. Inside looked dark as they stepped in from the sunlight, but once their eyes had adjusted to the gloom, Harrison could see there were candles all around the tiny single room chapel, and at the front was Finn laid out on the stone floor. Sitting on the wooden pews were the huddled shapes of several men. As Harrison and Cooper started down the aisle, the huddled shapes turned to look, giving features to the dark shadows.

'Morning, everyone. I'm sorry for your loss but I'd like everyone to come out please so that we can take statements and our forensics team can work,' DS Gibbons announced into the gloom.

There was a slight pause and then the men rose reluctantly and came towards them.

'It wasn't one of us. I know how you work, but it wasn't us,' a clean-shaven man with an ugly scar across his cheek, glared at DS Gibbons.

Harrison walked on down the aisle once everyone had left and placed the two boxes of forensic equipment on a pew not far from Finn's body. Gibbons joined him and the two of them approached the victim, keeping their distance so as not to contaminate any evidence that hadn't already been contaminated.

'Head injury,' Gibbons said. 'Looks like it cracked his skull, that was one heck of a wallop. He could have just fallen and cracked his head I suppose, so we need to see where he was found.'

Harrison's eyes scanned every inch of their victim, looking for the slightest clue.

'No, he fell forward onto grass,' he replied.

'Grass?'

'Yes you can see the staining on his knees and on his palm, there.'

They watched as a forensic officer moved to the body and started to bag the victim's hands in order to preserve any evidence that might have been caught under his fingernails.

'Rigor mortis?' Gibbons asked him.

'Yup, complete.'

'I'd say he was originally on his front, looks like some evidence of blood pooling in his skin,' Harrison added.

The forensic officer nodded in agreement and looked up at them both.

'Thanks, that's helpful,' Gibbons said thoughtfully. 'So probably killed sometime last night on those timings, by a blow to the side of his head. This could be completely unconnected to our burning, or it might have everything to do with it. Right, we'll have to wait for the pathologist to confirm everything, but in the meantime we need to start finding out who these men are and if any of them have a motive to kill.'

TWENTY-ONE

DS Gibbons went into full investigation mode once he'd exited the chapel.

'We need to conduct a murder investigation, and we are going to do so with, or without, your agreement,' he said to the assembled group of residents who'd left the chapel to stand outside. 'He was your friend, your leader, so I presume that I will have everyone's cooperation. You called us here to do a job and I will do my best to find out who did this.'

Harrison watched them all closely, looking at body language for any signals as to what might be going through their minds. They all looked dejected, sad. As you'd expect if your friend had been murdered.

None of them said a word to DS Gibbons and so he continued.

'Who found the victim?'

'Finn,' one of the men spoke up, 'his name was Finn.'

'My apologies,' Gibbons replied, 'can you please tell me who found Finn?'

'Me,' a large man with a bushy black and grey beard spoke up.

'What's your name?'

'Maggot.'

'OK, I'm very sorry, but you must all realise you are going to have to give me your full names please. I can easily take every one of your fingerprints and I'm sure I'll be able to get your details that way, so why don't you just make it easy on us all and not waste valuable time that could be spent tracking down a killer. Don't you want us to find out who killed your friend?'

'Daniel Ledger,' Maggot replied.

'Thank you, Daniel, could you please show me and my colleagues where it was that you found Finn?'

'Sure.'

Maggot started to move off. Gibbons spoke to one of the uniformed officers. 'Get some of my team up here, would you? I want everyone here's details and I want them questioned. Round up anyone else on the site. Where were they last night, and find out if any of them know Louise Swift, would you? And don't let any of them back inside that chapel.'

Harrison followed Maggot and was joined by the forensic officer he'd helped earlier, along with Gibbons.

'How many of you live here?' Gibbons asked their guide.

'Sixteen. Well it was sixteen.'

'And how do you all know each other?'

Maggot shrugged. 'We didn't. We just kind of heard about this place through word of mouth. Finn didn't let just anyone come here, you know. We all have a shared understanding as to how we want to live our lives.'

'Are you allowed to leave?'

'Yeah course. It's not some bloody secret cult, you know. Most of us don't have family, or at least family what want anything to do with us, so why would we? It's the only place I've called home, I'm at peace here. Well, we were.'

'I'm going to assume that you are all ex cons?' Gibbons asked slightly tentatively.

'Yeah, you assume right. Reformed ex cons. All of us wanted to turn our backs on crime. That ain't always easy when you're out there. You get labelled, stigmatised. You can't get a job or accommodation. We just want to live simple lives, that's it.'

'What do you do for money?'

'We sell some of what we grow, and we also make stuff. A couple of the lads learnt to do carpentry and woodwork while they was inside and we sell it. But we're pretty self-sufficient.'

'To the village?'

'No. The village don't like us. They look down on us. I ain't ever even been there, just kept clear of it. No, we go into the town.'

'How do you get there if you don't use cars?'

'We cycle. Got a little cart that goes on the back, bit like them kiddy carts that you see commuter parents using.'

'What about doctors?'

Maggot shrugged again. 'Not needed one so far. We use natural remedies where we can.'

'So did you know Louise Swift? I believe she did some natural herbal remedies.'

'No.'

'You never came across her at all?'

'I told you, no.'

'She was the young woman burnt to death in the field that your group rented.'

Maggot stopped and spun round.

'Is that what you're up to? You're trying to pin some woman's murder on us? The easy targets, a bunch of ex cons. Bound to be us, right? Well it weren't. None of us killed anyone. We did our time. We chose not to carry on that way of life.'

'I wasn't suggesting that you killed her, Mr Ledger, I just wondered if you or anybody had met her, if she'd ever come here?'

'No. No one came here. We don't encourage visitors. We just want to be left alone.'

They'd walked up the gravel driveway in between the agricultural area and the livestock, and come to the main house.

'He were round the back,' Maggot said to them, leading them round the side of the building.

The back of the house was a surprise after the front – it looked pretty much as you'd expect a mansion to. A walled garden was immediately in front and through the gate, they could see row upon row of herbs. Harrison made a note to go and have a look at what was in there. Some herbs were obviously used for cooking, but there were others that could have far more sinister or ritualistic uses. The lawn was a little less manicured than it would have been in its heyday with worn grass patches and scuffed clumps of earth. The football goals on either side, which had replaced the croquet hoops, explained why.

'He were just in front of the herb garden gate, lying face down on the lawn as though he'd tripped. Only when I got up to him, I saw the blood on his head. He was well gone.'

'Did it look to you as though he'd come out from the walled garden?'

'Looked that way. Sometimes he made chamomile tea when he couldn't sleep.'

'Did you find the herbs on the lawn near him?'

Maggot frowned. 'I don't remember. It was a shock, you know.'

'Of course. Thank you.'

'What about a torch?' Harrison asked.

Maggot shook his head. 'We don't have batteries. It was a light evening last night, the moon was strong. He knew his way.'

'If you don't mind, I'd like to ask you to go back to the others now,' Gibbons said to him. 'Is there anyone else in the house? If there is, could you get them to go and join the others at the chapel?'

'Are you arresting us?'

'No. I will probably want to speak to you again, but I just want to find out who killed Mr Smith and to do that I need to get as much information as possible from you all. You know how these things work.'

Maggot nodded sadly and sloped off into the house.

'Got a bit defensive about knowing Louise,' Gibbons remarked to Harrison. 'I didn't want to push it now, but we'll need to pull him in and have a more in-depth conversation. I'd like to know why he's lying.'

'There's a clear area here of flattened grass. I'll mark it up,' the forensic officer said to them. He'd been looking at the lawn where Maggot indicated he'd found Finn.

Harrison skirted around the lawn towards the entrance to the walled garden.

'There's some blood and some little flowers,' he heard the forensic officer say, 'I think they're chamomile.'

Harrison paused a few moments and turned to look back at the house. The killer had taken a risk. There must have been around thirty windows all looking out directly onto this lawn. Maggot said that Finn regularly came to get herbs to make his tea. Who but the residents would know that? Was this all a big coincidence, and Finn died because of an internal squabble? That was the easy answer. The obvious answer in a house filled with sixteen ex-prisoners. But was it the right one?

The path across the bottom of the lawn wasn't gravelled, but was instead just bare earth. Harrison shut out the chatter between Gibbons and the forensic officer and closed his eyes. He needed to try to work out what happened last night. Where Finn's killer had hidden and where he went after. He took some deep breaths in and then out again, focusing his mind, bringing all his senses together. Then he looked at the path. Finn had been barefoot – Harrison had noticed the dirt on his naked feet in the chapel – so first Harrison looked for where he had walked. It wasn't easy as the path was dusty and well-trodden, but he could see where Finn had walked across the lawn to the gateway of the walled garden and then back out again.

His attacker would have followed him and then made his escape. Harrison crouched down studying the grass along the edge of the lawn. There was no point going anywhere near to where Finn's body had been because even from here, Harrison could see that most, if not all, of the residents had gathered around it and trampled the ground. Most of the footprints went off in the direction of the house, but one set was at a diagonal – not towards the house or the entrance to the herb garden. Could this be the killer as they made their escape?

He followed the prints as they left the lawn and headed along the path towards the outer wall. The stride was long; it looked as though they were running not walking. They had been wearing trainers too. At this point, the outer wall was only a couple of hundred yards away. It was a tall wall, not one that could be easily scaled, but like the area around the entrance gate, there were plenty of trees that could be easily climbed and used to get over.

Harrison followed the footsteps right to the bottom of the wall. He looked up. There was no obvious way that someone could get up and over here. Had they brought something with them? Even Harrison couldn't scale a wall this height without help. He looked around for ideas and saw a tree about ten yards away. It was just set back a little too far into the garden to allow it to be used to get up the wall, but perhaps if he climbed it he might be able to see something.

Harrison took a short run and jumped high enough that when he grabbed hold of the lower branch, his huge biceps could pull him up. He climbed up higher until he could just see the top of the wall and beyond. Once there, he took a photograph of the spot. It could be worth looking on the other side to see if there was any evidence on the ground, and this would help him identify the right area. Then his eyes caught sight of some little white marks on the grey coping stones that ran along the top of the wall. Harrison used his phone to zoom in to them. They were fresh and they looked as though something, probably a metallic hook of some form, had dug into the stone. Just as it would if somebody had secured one of those rope ladders to the top in order to climb up and down. It gave him the possibility that somebody from outside had come into the Harmony House grounds. The question was, who and why?

TWENTY-TWO

Harrison rejoined Gibbons for a walk around Harmony House itself, getting a feel for how the men lived their lives and also hunting for Finn Smith's room. He focused on looking for any signs of religious extremism which could explain why someone in their group, or the group itself, could have targeted Louise Swift as a witch. He looked at books and notebooks, the pictures on the walls, and the very essence of how these men lived in the house. He could see nothing that gave any indications that they were people who thought that someone who was a psychic, was a witch.

'This is like looking for a needle in a haystack. If they want to hide something they've got a heck of a lot of places to secrete it,' Gibbons noted aloud.

The pair of them walked the length of the downstairs. Room after room, mostly relatively tidy and surprisingly well kept. Harrison paused in the grand hallway, where there was a guest book which seemed incongruous now that the house was closed to visitors. He looked inside and saw names that he recognised: Finn Smith, Daniel Ledger, Aaron Cooper, plus many others. Harrison took a photograph of those who had signed and counted how many there were after Finn. Twenty in total. That could mean that several of them had left.

'These guys all look to be forty plus, possibly lifetime criminals who, according to Mr Ledger, all wanted to go straight and live better lives. I suspect most of them would either be on the streets or risking being pulled back into crime if they weren't here,' Harrison mused.

'Yes. Or they could be running some kind of organised crime network from here. Sixteen criminals all working together.'

'You believe that?' Harrison turned to study Gibbons.

'We can't discount it. Wouldn't be the first time that a big house like this and its grounds have been used for criminal purposes.'

'But you just have to look around to see they must spend all their time keeping this place running. And there's no internet, no electricity, so something like a cannabis factory is out of the question...'

'So they say. Until we've searched the whole place, I'm going to stay open minded. I'd like to know where he got the money from to fund this place. If it's proceeds of crime...' Gibbons left the sentence unfinished. They both knew the result would be seizure if it was discovered that was what had happened. 'We are going to need to look thoroughly at what's going on here. Two deaths in the vicinity in just a few days and nobody saw or heard anything. That smacks of some kind of conspiracy to me.'

Gibbons stopped a moment to answer a call and Harrison took a minute to check his phone too. He'd felt it vibrate earlier, and hoped that it was Ryan with more information. He wasn't disappointed.

Finn Smith was Finn Montgomery, changed his name a year before he bought Harmony House.

Ryan had also sent through a newspaper report from the

trial. The story said Finn had apologised to the family of the victim and that the judge did consider he felt remorseful but a custodial sentence had to be given.

Harrison thought about the calm, controlled man who had met them at the gates. Had he really moved on from his criminal days, or was it an act just like his fake name, a surface change? He'd been pretty believable.

'They've got all fifteen residents at the chapel. None of them saw anything. The victim was with them last night and then they all went to bed. First they knew of it was when Ledger raised the alarm. At least, that's what they say. Of course they've had plenty of time to get their stories straight before inviting us here. Several hours in fact. Let's check upstairs while they're at the chapel.'

The bedroom doors all handily carried the name of their occupants. Harrison and Gibbons checked in each one, making sure everybody was really accounted for. They had to go to the next floor up to find Finn Smith's room. It was smaller than the others, probably originally servant's quarters.

'Bloody hell, he lived like a monk,' Gibbons said as they stood in the doorway. The room didn't even have carpets or rugs; it was just a bed and a set of drawers. No mirror, no luxuries.

'I don't think it was religion that drove his lifestyle,' Harrison said, surveying the scene.

'There's still the chance that Louise's killers murdered her due to their religious beliefs; maybe they're hiding something,' Gibbons countered.

'Yes, but if the residents here took umbrage with her talents as a medium and psychic, then I've not seen any evidence that it has anything to do with religion. Not unless one of them is a closet fundamentalist or they've got a hidden cellar and cave system where they practise some kind of religious fanaticism. But that's not what I'm seeing when I look in this room. I think for Finn this was all about personal atonement. Someone died after his last burglary and the only decoration in this room is that newspaper cutting over there.' Harrison nodded at the far wall.

Gibbons moved across the room to take a look. 'You're right. Father of three, Rajesh Varma, died after suffering a heart attack following a break-in to his family business. Mr Varma was taken to hospital but died two days later.' Gibbons turned back to Harrison. 'How did you know that?'

'My assistant just texted to say Finn changed his name a year before buying this place and we know that he'd been convicted of burglary and manslaughter twelve years ago.'

'Could be someone getting revenge. I'll get the team to check out the family, what was he called originally?'

'Finn Montgomery.'

Gibbons made a note and then opened the drawers one by one. Inside were just various items of clothing, all neatly folded. Harrison looked around too but found nothing that indicated the personality of the man other than that he was disciplined and lived a frugal life. Through the bedroom window he could see the forensic officer combing the area of lawn where Finn's life had ended. Despite his past, there was something that Harrison found quite sad about his death. From what he could see, it looked like Finn really had tried to turn over a new leaf and was helping others to do the same. Why, then, should someone want to kill him?

They found nothing else in Finn's room that could help them and so returned to the gardens where officers could be seen scouring the grounds.

'Good little set up here.' Harrison nodded to the animals and crops in front of them.

'Very *The Good Life*,' Gibbons said looking at him, and then noticed Harrison's nonplussed face. 'Ah suppose that was well before your time!'

'I'm not sure what you're referring to,' Harrison replied.

'TV comedy show about a couple who turned their suburban garden into a smallholding, it's from the mid-seventies, but it's often on reruns,' Gibbons replied.

'I don't really watch TV,' Harrison said to him, missing the eyebrow raise from Gibbons.

'Sir,' a shout distracted them from behind.

Gibbons and Harrison walked back to the house where an officer was walking towards them, looking flushed.

'I think you need to see this, sir,' he said, beckoning them into the house. 'It's in their fire pit out back there.'

Harrison and Gibbons walked through the hallway and kitchen and back out into the garden. To the left was a seating area and a fire pit had been dug into the ground.

'That must be where they were sitting last night,' Gibbons said. 'What have you got?'

'Mobile phone, sir.'

They came to a stop at the edge of the fire pit and looked down amongst the ash. The phone was in the middle, blackened and screen cracked. Gibbons bent down, not to pick it up but to get a closer look.

Gibbons nodded. 'But they say they don't have mobile phones here, and why burn it? It looks like it's just been tossed in.'

'Surely the battery would have exploded in the heat?' Harrison said to him.

'Good point. It hasn't, so that suggests that it was taken out prior to the phone being put in the fire. We still haven't found Louise Swift's mobile. Get the forensics team to bag this ASAP and let's see what we've got. I want this whole place turned upside down. If this is her phone, then we might find the laptop too.'

Gibbons stood up straight and rubbed his lower back absentmindedly. 'So, what's gone on here then? Did one of the men, perhaps Maggot, kill Louise because she knew something that she was going to use against them? Did Finn find out and so he had to be silenced? I know it's the easy solution here, but we can't ignore the fact that we're dealing with a group of convicted criminals. This all looks very nice on the surface, but are we looking at a facade for something else? I'm not sure I'm buying all this wanting to turn over a new leaf business. We've got two murders and we know that Louise had mentioned Harmony House in her letters to Zack. This lot have had hours to clear up before calling us in over Finn's murder. How do we know they're not a group of misogynistic nutters who think all women should be burnt at the stake?' Gibbons turned to Harrison. 'You found ritualistic symbols and we know her death was staged like a witch burning, what do you think?'

'I think that if these men had killed Louise and stolen her phone and laptop, they'd have cleared up that mobile phone before we arrived because as you said they had hours to prepare.'

'Maybe they forgot, maybe they hadn't meant to kill Finn and then went into panic mode. Or maybe they were just too busy covering something else up.'

'Then why call us at all?'

'Hmm, true. We'd be none the wiser until we arrived asking to see him again.'

'At which point they could have just said he'd gone away.'

'So, none of this makes any sense unless they need him dead. Perhaps they plan to sell this place and split the proceeds between them. That's a solid motive, but why Louise Swift? What are we missing here?'

Harrison and Gibbons returned to the incident room to update the team and to get across all the information that was coming in. When they had left Harmony House, reinforcements were just arriving to conduct fingertip searches of the grounds and the house. It was going to take more than just one day to get the whole area cleared and so Gibbons needed to talk to his superiors about moving or containing the remaining fifteen men at Harmony House in order to preserve the crime scene. When he'd suggested to them moving to a hotel earlier, he had been met with a chorus of complaints, not least the fact that someone had to stay to look after the animals. It was a headache he could have done without but it needed sorting, so while Gibbons got on with coming up with a solution, Harrison decided to take another look at all the statements that had been taken from the villagers, and the new ones from the Harmony House men.

Harrison had just settled into reading them, when some of the detectives who'd been up to Harmony House returned. He could hear the criminal records of the various residents being read out.

'This one was a pyromaniac. Used to do insurance jobs, set

countless fires that were made to look like accidents but weren't,' he heard one officer say. 'Wouldn't take him long to get a good bonfire going.'

'Blackmailer and fraudster,' another officer retorted, 'and looky here, manslaughter and public disorder.'

Harrison could almost see the minds of the team being made up as to who was responsible for the two murders. The investigation ran the danger of being turned from a hunt for a killer of a suspected witch, to being a witch hunt in itself.

'OK, everyone, a quick check-in please,' Gibbons clapped his hands and shouted to the room. Everyone fell silent. 'The boss is coming in half an hour and will be holding a press conference. I don't need to tell you all that you do not speculate to anybody about the two murders. At present we don't know if they are connected, but as they're so close together in geography and time, we are treating them as such, for now. It's possible that the Harmony House murder may get taken off us by another team, but only if we can find no links between the two. I still want to know where our victim, Finn Smith, formerly known as Finn Montgomery, got his money from. Chase down his bank records. This is critical. Any red flags with the background checks on the villagers?'

'Still working through them boss, nothing so far.'

'What about the Community Church? Any previous incidences with them? Do we know when they set up and if they were based anywhere else?'

'Started twelve years ago in London. There's a few minor incidents when they demonstrated outside abortion clinics and the like, and eventually it appears the landlord of the property kicked them out after the windows were repeatedly smashed in and graffiti daubed on the walls. They then moved out of the city where they could afford to buy a place of their own, hence why they arrived in Thistleford.'

'Anything to link them to Louise? She lived in London as well.'

'No nothing, sir, and they were in north London so not in the same neighbourhood.'

'OK, keep digging, and, Luke, can you try getting hold of Charley Jones again. She wasn't in when I tried, and we need to speak to her about her connections with the Community Church. In the meantime, start working on the Harmony House men and check if there are any connections between them all, that especially includes Louise Swift. We believe that she knew Daniel Ledger, who goes by the name of Maggot. It was Ledger who claims to have found Finn Smith's body in the early hours of this morning. Focus on him, I want to know everything about him.'

'We've got professional fire setters and a murderer among the Harmony House lot,' one officer said, raising his eyebrows.

'Doesn't mean to say they're who we are looking for,' Gibbons replied, much to Harrison's relief. 'Keep an open mind. All of you, but let's make sure we thoroughly check out the obvious ones. Remember that whoever did that to Louise couldn't have been working alone. We are looking for a group of individuals.'

There were a few murmurs in the room and then the team got back to their work. The noise level was still high and when Gibbon's boss arrived with his own entourage, the demand on space grew even more critical. Harrison couldn't concentrate with the noise and so he took his laptop and went down the street to the café where he'd met Gibbons earlier – and where he could concentrate.

He chose himself a seat in the far corner of the little café. Compared to the incident room, it was positively blissful in here. The only sounds were the quiet murmurs of people talking, or the hiss and clink as cups of coffee were made and handed over. He ordered himself a mint tea and bought a flapjack for a quick sugar boost. At least the oats were healthy.

He started by reading through each of the villagers' statements. With each one, he mentally pictured their homes along the one street that ran through the village, their proximity to Louise Swift's cottage and if possible their faces. He'd not met them all and so the latter wasn't as easy, but it was what they said that mattered. The photograph of Charley Jones at the Community Church kept coming into his mind. Young minds could be particularly influenced by men like Pastor Sam, especially if she was going through a period of feeling unsure of who she was and where she was going in life. He'd feel a whole lot better if he knew that Charley was safely at home with her mother.

Once he'd read the villagers' statements, he moved on to the Harmony House ones. There was a marked difference in the tone. He could almost hear the defensiveness of the men in their clipped sentences, no doubt slightly improved on by the officer taking the statement, but none the less, direct and clearly resentful of the fact they were having to give the statements at all. The villagers, on the other hand, were all about the shock of what had happened to Louise and each and every one gushed about how much they had liked her and appreciated her psychic gifts.

There was another thing they all had in common. None of them had seen or heard a thing relating to either murder.

Harrison sent Ryan the list of names of both the villagers and the Harmony House men. He also asked him to run the statements through some software that Ryan had told him about. He'd noticed something else about them that was interesting. With the statements read and his mint tea just a green stain in the bottom of his mug, Harrison wanted to get on with the next part of his investigation and for that he'd need to get into Louise Swift's cottage.

. . .

'Words got out about the Harmony House murder,' Gibbons said to him the second he arrived back in the incident room. 'We've not even announced it officially, the press conference is in an hour, but we've already got protestors and social media ghouls outside their gates. Could turn into yet another crowd situation. I need to go into a meeting with the tactical support team. Do you need anything to help with your investigation?'

'I'd like to get back into Louise's cottage.'

'OK, let me text Oliver in forensics now. I think you should be alright for this afternoon. You might need to just go and pick up the key from him at Harmony House.' Gibbons typed into his phone. 'Anything else you've noticed that we can use?' Gibbons asked hopefully.

Harrison looked at his own phone quickly to see if Ryan had managed to run the statements through. He hadn't.

'I'll talk to you later,' he said to the detective, aware that he was on a tight schedule, 'there's just a few things I need to check out first. I'm going to spend some time getting to know Louise Swift.'

'Oliver says you're free to go into the cottage, but he's got the key because he had to go straight up to Harmony House.'

'No problem, I'll go and fetch it. There was something I wanted to check out there anyway and we didn't get time earlier.'

'OK, and Luke spoke to Mrs Jones again. She said that Charley was with a friend and she'd let us know when she got back.'

'With a friend?' Harrison queried.

'Yeah I know. I've asked him to chase it up again and get an address because I'm fully aware that Charley is the one who probably knows more about Louise's business than anyone.'

'She could be in danger.'

'I'll escalate it.'

Harrison's unease over the Church and what might have happened to Charley Jones, dominated his mind, but there were other ideas forming too and he needed to see if there was evidence that backed them up. His mantra of looking at the facts and using them to formulate a hypothesis, rather than using his own or someone else's suppositions and then searching for evidence to back them up, was being tested. He had to push his own prejudices from his mind, just as he wanted the rest of the team to do. He had to focus on the facts.

TWENTY-FOUR

Harrison rode up to Harmony House on his bike, managing to weave slowly around the people walking on the lanes. He went past the field where Louise had been murdered on the bonfire, the acrid smell of burnt wood now just a hint in the air. While the bonfire had been packaged up and cleared away to a warehouse for forensics, two officers still stood sentry at the field gate, ensuring that the site remained free of ghoulish sightseers.

Instead of going up to the main gate, Harrison continued round the perimeter wall until he reached the area that he calculated would be adjacent to the walled garden. He got off his bike and looked at the photograph he'd taken of the wall, searching for the trees which were in the image. Once he'd located them, he walked across the grass verge to the perimeter of the wall, scanning the ground as he went.

If he was right, he'd find some signs that somebody had been there on this side. At first he couldn't see anything, and so he'd retraced back to the roadside, looking for a possible entry point. With the ground so hard, and it being the day after, it wasn't easy to see the footprints, but he found them amongst the damage to the grass and the daisies which smothered the verge.

From here it was just a case of following the footsteps to the base of the wall where he found an area that had been flattened, possibly by whatever was used to get the killer over the wall being placed on the ground, and then the perpetrator's body weight as they dropped back down. Harrison looked all around, but there were no handy clues dropped by Finn's killer, just the ghost of his presence in the crushed grass and daisies.

Harrison logged the spot with GPS and took a couple more photographs, then returned to his bike and made the journey back down the road to Harmony House's gate. Crowd barriers had been put up in the area outside the gate so that police vehicles could be parked. Harrison showed his ID to the officer manning the barricade in order to leave his bike out of the way. There were around twenty people there, some simply taking photographs, while a small group of women seemed to be chanting, their eyes shut as they sat cross-legged and holding hands on the ground.

Instead of one of Harmony House's usual bearded gatekeepers, a clean-shaven police officer was on duty at the gate, logging those going in and out. Harrison showed his ID again and then dialled Oliver's mobile to find out where he was so that he could get the key.

By the time Harrison had walked to the back garden and collected the key for Louise's cottage, the day was showing signs of slipping into darkness. He told Oliver about the place on the wall where he believed someone had come over and the forensic officer sent one of his team to take a look. It was going to be difficult to find any evidence that would identify who it was, but at least it set the principle that an external individual had come into the grounds the night that Finn was killed.

There was a police officer still on duty outside Louise's cottage, part of the 24/7 security they'd had to put in place since the killing in order to protect their crime scenes from overzealous social media investigators or journalists.

Harrison signed in and then stepped back into Louise's world. For a few moments he stood quietly in the hallway, centring his mind and body and focusing. He listened to the sounds of the cottage, a faint murmur of a television just audible through the hallway wall into Violet's living room where she must be sat with the volume turned up loud so that she could hear. Harrison breathed in deeply, taking in the scent of the place, of the woman who had lived here. Scented oils had been used, no doubt to create an atmosphere, their aroma still evident in the soft fabrics and furnishings.

He closed his eyes and imagined Louise living here. He had a different view of her from the last time he'd visited. She was more rounded in his mind. A woman who had come alive through the words she'd written to her boyfriend in prison. Before she'd just been a video personality, trying to get people into parting with their cash for a tarot or spirit reading. Louise had what his mother would have called, the gift of the gab. If you'd given her a stick she'd have persuaded you that you really needed it by making up a story about how important it was to have in your life.

Some of that skillset was innate, but some she'd clearly practised and developed. Some would no doubt see it as a gift, or perhaps magic, sorcery, or witchcraft. But like 99.9% of things that Harrison investigated, there was a logical and practical human reason behind them all.

When he'd watched the videos of her on TikTok, there were some things he'd seen that he'd not spotted when he and Ross Gibbons had looked around quickly that first day. Harrison needed to get back in to look for them, or to confirm that they were missing. The latter could provide him with the motive for her murder.

He pulled out his phone and found the video Louise had

recorded where she showed her fans the little sitting room, or her 'reading room' as she'd called it. She'd scanned the bookshelves, allowing the viewer to see the titles of the spines. Most of the books had been either piled on the floor, or put back onto the shelf by the forensic and investigative team. Harrison looked through every single one. There were three books he'd seen right at the end of the shot, books that she'd tried to skip over, and these weren't there.

The other item that she'd shown her viewers was what she'd called her spirit slates. Harrison knew exactly what these were for. They were an old trick used to fool people into believing that they were receiving messages from a loved one beyond the grave. She would have got the person to write a message on a slip of paper to their loved one and asked them to slip it between the two slates which she'd already shown them were blank. When she'd performed a little bit of convening with the spirit, she would have opened the slates again revealing a message in reply to their question – except she had written it earlier and the slates could be manipulated so that the message was originally hidden. It was an easy, straightforward trick. The slates were clearly visible in her video, but despite searching everywhere, Harrison couldn't find them.

He texted Oliver, the forensics officer, and asked him if they'd removed any items like this from the cottage.

While he waited for his answer, he looked in the little drawer of the table where Louise sat for the readings. Inside he found some wires that would have had something plugged into them, and a switch. Whatever it was had gone, but Harrison got down onto his knees and looked under the table. There was a funnel shape which pointed towards the client, and a hole in the back of the drawer that led into it. He couldn't be sure, but he suspected that when Louise conjured her spirits, she would have turned on some kind of fan that would have given the feeling of a chill presence arriving.

What was still in the drawer, were some pre-folded pieces of paper. One of the most basic tricks, known as the billet trick. She would have asked people to write a word in the centre of the paper, possibly she may have used a pen to create a circle and asked them to write in that circle to make sure they wrote it where she wanted it. Then she would have ripped it up in front of them and given the pieces back to them, or perhaps burnt them in the flames of a candle. Either way it didn't matter. She would speak to the spirits and they would tell her what the word was that the person had written. Only of course, it was all a trick. The paper was torn up but in a specific way which meant the part that had the writing on it was still intact and Louise would have used some sleight of hand to conceal it in her palm and read it.

Then Harrison went into the kitchen and looked at the herbs and 'magic potions' that she'd been creating. He had no video evidence of the kitchen prior to the day of her murder but when he'd looked around with DS Gibbons, he'd seen a carrier bag with several packets of paracetamol in them. That and the residue of white powder in the pestle dish had raised his suspicions. This time he looked more closely and also found labels already written with various ailments on them, ready to give to unsuspecting clients who were no doubt charged a fortune. She could have killed someone if they were allergic to the painkillers she'd secreted into the mixture.

Harrison's phone buzzed in his pocket.

> Nothing removed yet due to the security in place, but due to remove items in the next 24 hours.

Harrison wrote back:

> Have the contents of her pestle bowl been tested?

No. We can arrange that if you think it's
important.

Yes please.

The fact that nothing had been taken by the investigative team was incredibly crucial knowledge because it indicated that whoever did this to Louise's cottage and killed her, had removed more than just her laptop.

Finally, Harrison stepped into her office. It had been 'tidied' of sorts. Forensic and investigative officers had sorted through everything and paperwork was now piled and labelled, no doubt ready to be taken to the police station as evidence. Harrison crossed to a pile of local newspapers which had been tossed to one side as not being important. When he opened the paper at the obituary column, he found exactly what he'd suspected. She not only targeted the vulnerable online, but she'd also sought out the newly bereaved locally.

The woman had no shame. She'd underlined the ads where there was a widow or widower mentioned, and no doubt turned up at funerals, watched and worked out when she should pounce, just like she'd done with Mrs Wilson. It was an old scam, to watch the target for a day or so and then 'accidentally' come across them in the street. She'd have said something about their deceased spouse sending their love or saying sorry and that would have got her the 'in'. After that it was just a case of arranging a private and no doubt expensive session where she could carry on conning the bereaved person that she had been contacted by their loved one and told to speak to them. Zack had told them earlier that it had been a fake séance which had caused her troubles in London. She'd obviously tricked the wrong person's mother or father and passed on a message that she shouldn't have known. She'd clearly not learned her lesson.

Finding any other evidence was going to be difficult. Louise would have done most of her research online and Harrison suspected that she would have done 'warm readings', where armed with the name of the person she was talking to, she'd have tried to find out some basic things about them. Most people were so trusting on social media, sharing their photographs and life stories. Even little details could create the illusion of her having clairvoyant or spiritualist powers, but more often than not people would post on their Facebook accounts if they'd lost a loved one or were facing other life challenges, and that gave her enough ammunition to fool her clients hook, line, and sinker.

Louise Swift was neither a clairvoyant, nor a witch. She was a con woman who was very skilled at reading people, their body language and facial expressions. She'd found a way to dupe innocent people into believing she had special powers. The question was, who believed her so much that they would burn her as a witch, or was there something else behind the motive for murder?

TWENTY-FIVE

After looking around Louise's cottage, Harrison had gone straight back to the hotel where he'd booked in again, eaten, and headed to bed. It had been a full and busy day and he was tired, but he had to check his emails and see if Ryan needed him or had found anything that could help him with the current inquiry.

There was a request for information following a spate of chicken killings. Bodies of chickens which looked to have been killed as part of some sort of ritual, had been found on the outskirts of a park in Birmingham. Harrison looked at the photographs, and the other evidence which had been found and confirmed to the force dealing with the case, that it was some form of ritualistic offering, probably as part of the Santeria religion. He copied in Ryan and asked him to send the officers some information which would help them identify the kinds of communities who might be carrying out the practices.

Ryan had also sent him links to a few more videos of Louise that he'd found online, and the news stories around her murder. He knew his boss well and suspected that Harrison wouldn't have watched any news himself.

Harrison watched the news reports. He'd meant to catch them a couple of days ago when he'd seen a couple of the villagers being interviewed. Hearing what they said publicly about Louise and her murder was as important as reading their statements. The couple he'd seen turned out to be the next-door neighbours, Laura and Jim Burrows. Jim took up most of the time, waxing lyrical about how wonderful Louise had been, using her talents to help ease the gout that had made his feet so painful. Harrison thought back to the pestle and mortar in her kitchen and the ibuprofen and paracetamol which had been in the shopping bag. There was also an interview with Nick Rogers, who said that as head of the village, he was going to suggest they create some kind of monument to celebrate Louise's life and her incredible gift, which had been taken from them.

Harrison lay back on the bed thinking about all the people who had been in Louise's life and what she had meant to them. To some, she was merely a hustler who took money from those who were feeling vulnerable, but to others, she gave hope at the most difficult times of their lives. Wasn't that what many religions did? Wasn't that helping people in some way? If a widow like Violet thought her long-dead husband was talking to her, that would give her joy and hope that they would one day be reunited. What price could you put on that? Then to others, Louise was evil. Deceiving people. Acting against God's will and doing the devil's work. Did one of those relationships end in her death? Why the elaborate ritual of the stoning and bonfire if revenge and anger were merely the catalysts. There were far less dramatic and public ways of killing someone.

Harrison was tired after yet another busy day concentrating and the previous two nights of disturbed sleep. He understood the importance of sleep, not only so that he could concentrate to the best of his abilities the next day, but also so his mind could process all the information that he'd taken in since he'd woken up. He got ready for bed and turned the light off, but the faces and voices kept spinning around his head as he tried to find the motive for Louise's murder and quell the rising unease that Tanya was drifting away from him.

Harrison was pleased to wake up to his alarm in the morning and find he'd slept soundly all night. He knocked back a glass of water, jumped in the shower and then headed down to breakfast, his mind already buzzing with ideas.

Halfway through eating, DS Gibbons called him. He was making a habit of interrupting breakfast.

'Harrison, are you coming in this morning?'

'Yes, just eating breakfast then I'll head straight in.'

'Lucky you. I've been up since six this morning after somebody spray-painted the boundary wall at Harmony House with the word "*Murderers*" and apparently the press has been flying drones and helicopters overhead to get photographs of the secret sect of convicted killers who live in luxury behind the gates of a stately home. I quote from headlines there! It's a right shitshow again. And we've still got religious groups praying up at the field. I could do with a good dose of sanity in all this. Planning a briefing this morning to go over what we've found so far. Did you glean anything more from Louise's cottage?'

'As a matter of fact, I did.'

'Good. Briefing in one hour. Can you be there?'

'Definitely.'

Forty-five minutes later, Harrison walked into the incident room. He expected to find DS Gibbons there, but was instead met with a scene more reminiscent of the *Marie Celeste*.

'What's going on, is the briefing being held somewhere else?' he asked the young, uniformed officer who'd clearly been told to man the phones.

'They've gone up to Harmony House to arrest someone.'

'Why, on what basis?'

'They found some evidence. Wood that matched the bonfire, a bag with black spray paints like was used in her cottage, a can with diesel in it, and what looks like a part of Louise's laptop. Plus that mobile phone which was found yesterday has come back as being highly likely to be hers from the serial number. They're pulling in some bloke who's a convicted killer, he had her business card in his room, so they're gonna see what he says.'

'So it's in relation to the killing of Louise Swift, not Finn?'

'Yeah.'

Harrison's heart sank. He could be wrong, but he didn't think that he was. The investigation team had opted for the easy targets and maybe somebody was helping them do that.

He didn't have to wait long to find out more information because DS Gibbons marched into the room about five minutes later.

'Harrison, we've pulled in Daniel Ledger. He lied yesterday when he said he'd never heard of Louise Swift. We knew that anyway from what she'd told Zack, but we also found one of her cards in his room, so he definitely met up with her. I don't think they're telling us the whole truth. They've all clammed up since yesterday. I thought he was going to punch the officer who asked him to come down here to help us with our enquiries. He got quite abusive so we ended up arresting him.'

Harrison said nothing. He thought about Daniel Ledger, the man they called Maggot, what he'd said about their group and how he'd found peace at last in his life, and he wondered if DS Gibbons and his team had just made a very big mistake.

Gibbons looked up at him, no doubt wondering why he hadn't answered.

'Do you want to observe the interview?' Gibbons asked. 'He's in with his brief now so we should be ready to talk to him pretty soon.'

'Yes, please,' Harrison replied and followed Gibbons out of the incident room and into the bowels of the police station.

Maggot was sat in a small room, a scowl stamped on his face, arms crossed and a defiant look in his eyes. Sitting next to him was a man in a navy suit that looked as though he'd bought it when he was a good few pounds lighter. When DS Gibbons walked into the interview room with another officer, Maggot instantly got defensive.

'You said you were there to find Finn's killer and now you pull this stunt!'

'Mr Ledger, I'm not pulling any stunts, I'm just trying to get to the bottom of what's been going on round here.'

'We're under bloody siege that's what's going on. Do you know people have been trying to get over the wall and into our grounds? All we asked was to be left alone.'

Harrison was watching the interview on a video feed in a room down the corridor, but he could feel the indignation and anger coming off Daniel Ledger.

'I'm sorry, we are doing our best to control the public. It's been an issue from the start.' Gibbons sighed. He went through the formalities of the interview process and started the recording.

'Mr Ledger, we are recording this interview so I want you to first of all tell me how you knew Louise Swift.'

'I didn't know her.'

'OK, I am going to show you this business card which was found in your bedroom at Harmony House.'

Maggot leaned forward to look at the small piece of card in the plastic envelope. He let out a frustrated sigh and shook his head.

'I met her once, that's all. We walk around the fields and lanes collecting kindling and wood and we bumped into her one day. Can't lie and say that it wasn't nice talking to an attractive young woman, but then she said some stuff about my past and my dead mum, and it got me thinking. She told me she could put me in touch with my mum. There's stuff I always wanted to say to her, you know, stuff that I never got to say cos I was inside, and she said a few things that made me think maybe my mum had spoken to her. Pathetic I know, but when someone stops you like that, at random, it catches you off guard. Anyways, she gave me her card and I put it in my pocket; but then she started talking about me and how I'd been in prison and stuff and I started to get suspicious. Eventually she came clean and told me that I'd shared a cell with her dad a few years back. So then she tells me that she had some big bluff that she reckoned would make a packet but she needed a bit of help. I told her we'd all turned our backs on crime and weren't interested. She didn't appreciate that. When I told Finn later, he said she'd also approached him and he'd told her where to go. I never saw her again and forgot I still had her card.'

'Why didn't you tell me this yesterday?'

'Because of the whole reason why I'm sitting here now. I thought you'd instantly blame the ex con for her murder and I wasn't going to give you that opportunity. I never knew her. I just bumped into her once.'

'Did she give you any more detail about the nature of this bluff?'

'No. I didn't give her the opportunity. Didn't want to know.'

'What about Finn, did she tell him?'

'He didn't give me all the details, but said it was something to do with the big bloke in the village. That's all I know.'

Harrison had been staring at the screen on which he was watching the interview, looking at Maggot's body language and facial expressions, as well as the tone in his voice. What he saw, told him that Maggot was being honest. What he said, he believed happened.

DS Gibbons, however, had more up his sleeve.

'Can you explain to us how we found old wooden fence panels in your wood pile, that match those that were used in the bonfire?'

'We collect wood from all over the area. They were probably from the dump pile that the villagers use.'

'Dump pile?'

'Yeah, in the little woods, just outside of the village, there's an area where they dump stuff that can rot. Stuff like wooden fence panels and garden waste, as well as tree branches that have been cut down and the like. We always check it when we're looking for wood because it's easy pickings.'

'Can you show me on a map where that pile is?'

'Sure.'

DS Gibbons brought up a Google map of the area on his phone. 'Whereabouts, in this wood?'

'Shit I ain't ever used that kind of a map before. Where's that toffee-nosed bloke's house? The one who thinks he's better than everyone else. It's on the edge of his land.'

DS Gibbons manipulated the map so that Maggot could get his bearings.

'There,' he said pointing with his finger at the map where Nick Rogers's house and land gave way to trees. It's a huge pile of stuff. Some of it is too big for us to carry back in our cart. We just take the small stuff.'

'Thank you, we'll check that out. Now can you explain to me why we found a diesel can and a carrier bag with black spray paint in one of the Harmony House garden sheds?'

'Diesel? What? No way. None of us would have brought that onto the site, Finn would have gone mad. We don't need it, there's nothing that uses diesel.'

'Whoever lit the bonfire that killed Louise Swift, used diesel. We are getting it tested now to see if it's the same batch.'

Maggot swore, but said nothing further.

'You should also know that we found the remains of a mobile phone in the fire pit that you were all sat around the night before Finn's murder. We also discovered a part of Louise's laptop in the same carrier bag that had the diesel in. How do you explain that?'

'You are kidding me. It's obvious some bastard is trying to frame us. Do you really think that if we'd done it, we'd be that bloody stupid to leave the items where you could find them?'

'Maybe you thought they were safe because it's a restricted access property?'

'No. I'm telling you, that's bullshit.' Maggot looked to his solicitor. 'It weren't me or any one of us.'

'Nobody else is allowed on your land, Mr Ledger, how could somebody have got access?'

'Well obviously somebody can. It's not bloody impenetrable you know. Somebody clearly got in and killed Finn. Haven't you seen them bloody kids trying to get photos and videos. They sit on top of the wall and taunt us.'

'Or perhaps one of you was responsible for Louise's murder and Finn Smith found out and confronted them. Perhaps that's why he was killed.'

'No way, man. No way. None of us would hurt Finn. He's helped every one of us. He's the reason why some of us are still alive. This is a complete fix up, that's what this is. What are you doing to find out who really killed him? Why aren't you looking as hard for his killer, or does he not matter so much as he's an ex con and not some pretty young woman?'

'Mr Ledger, I can assure you that he does matter every bit as much and we are continuing our investigations. It doesn't help us if you and your friends are secretive and don't give us information.'

'Yeah well, not surprisingly most of us don't exactly trust you lot, as you've proven today. You gonna charge me or take me home?' Daniel Ledger stood up.

'I'm not going to charge you, Mr Ledger, we can give you a lift back home. But you need to have a good think how items from Louise's home, along with those used in her killing, were found on Harmony House land.'

TWENTY-SIX

Half an hour after Maggot had been taken back to Harmony House, the two police officers who'd been dispatched to check out the dump pile in the trees near Nick Rogers's house, came back to the incident room with their findings. Harrison had been sitting brooding, thinking about the events so far that morning.

'There's nothing there,' he heard one of them say to DS Gibbons.

'Nothing there? So he was lying?'

'We're not sure, sir, but there's nothing there now.' The officer shrugged and the pair of them looked at each other.

Harrison was already feeling wound-up about what he'd heard in the interview and this was the last straw. He walked out the incident room without a word and got on his bike to head straight to the woods where the dump pile should have been. He could see the way the inquiry was leading and he wasn't convinced it was in the right direction.

. . .

A slight mist had started to descend when he arrived on the short track that led to the site. Harrison didn't ride his bike down the track. He could see where the two police officers had driven down, but he didn't want to obliterate any further evidence of tyre marks and so instead he got off his bike and walked the rest of the way.

As he went, he scanned the ground and the surrounding undergrowth for signs of activity. He expected to find something, and he wasn't disappointed. There was clear evidence that some kind of vehicle had been up and down the track flattening the earth, before the police car had driven down it earlier.

Harrison didn't just look down, but also up. He saw tree branches and bushes that had damage to their tips where something large had gone past and ripped at them. By the time he reached the area where the dump pile had been, it was more than obvious that while it looked clear, there had been significant activity in the area. There was a small clearing and towards the back of it, a large patch of earth that was devoid of any undergrowth. It had been scraped and flattened, traces of what looked like garden waste mixed into the soil along with the odd plastic plant tag. There had definitely been a pile of something here, but somebody had moved it.

Harrison could see that the tracks for the mechanical vehicle went off down the muddy trail in the opposite direction to the entrance and so he followed them. It took him towards the edge of the band of trees where there were fields with horses grazing. This must be Nick Rogers's land. He didn't hesitate, but continued following the tracks across a grassy area and towards a metal lean-to barn. It was locked.

Harrison walked around its perimeter until he found a small gap through which he could peer. It was difficult to see inside because it was dark, but there was no mistaking the machinery that was in there. He pulled out his phone and dialled DS Gibbons.

While he waited for the detective to join him, Harrison brought up Google Earth and zoomed in to the clearing in the woods. There, unmistakably was a large pile of something brown and green. He walked back to meet Gibbons.

'What you got for me then? Suppose you're going to tell me those two young officers didn't look properly?'

'Well, they looked, but didn't see,' Harrison said.

Gibbons humphed.

'Firstly, I took a look at the tracks here.' Harrison pointed to the muddy track. 'There's been a heavy piece of machinery driven up and down flattening the ground. You can see where the police car travelled down it earlier, and you can also see where the machinery snagged the bushes and some of the branches overhead.' Harrison indicated what he'd spotted.

Gibbons said nothing, just nodded and followed him.

'This was where the pile was. The ground has been dug over and then flattened back down again. On Google Earth there's a clear mound of something brown and green here.' He held out his phone to show the detective the image he'd snapped.

Gibbons peered at it. 'It's quite pixelated, but yeah, I can see that it could be the shape of what looks like wood on top.'

'I followed the machinery tracks, they lead out of the clearing and across the field to a barn where I can see something large parked inside,' Harrison continued.

Harrison turned and looked at Gibbons to see how he was taking the revelations.

'The tracks, do they match what we saw up at the field?'

'They look pretty similar to me.'

The two of them walked along and across the field where Gibbons peered into the gloom, just as Harrison had done earlier.

'OK, I'll get one of the forensic guys down here. We'll need to look at that equipment. If they did use that there could possibly be traces of Louise's DNA on it. Thanks, Harrison.'

Harrison acknowledged his appreciation.

Gibbons paused before continuing.

'You don't think it's the Harmony House men, do you? I could tell you didn't approve of pulling Daniel Ledger in.'

'It's not about approval, I just think it's a waste of time.'

'OK, so tell me your theory. You think the Community Church is involved?'

'I had my suspicions about them, they certainly tick all the boxes and I'm concerned that it's some kind of a cult being built there, but I don't think religion was the motive in Louise's murder. It's what the killers wanted us to believe, but it was almost too textbook.' What Harrison didn't say to DS Gibbons was that his own experiences had led him towards the initial rookie detective mistake of confirmation bias. He'd seen echoes of his past in Pastor Sam, and although he had concerns for the people in his congregation, there was nothing that connected them to Louise apart from Charley Jones and she'd reportedly left the Church nearly two years ago. He'd been looking for and selecting evidence that confirmed his own prior beliefs and not looking at it objectively.

Harrison stopped a moment and looked at the detective. 'Did you notice anything about the villagers' statements?' he asked Gibbons.

'I've not read them all yet, what is it that you spotted?'

'It's like they've all rehearsed the same story. Most of them have a seventy-five per cent compatibility which is only achievable if they all agreed to say the same things. Jenny Hall at the shop, Nick Rogers, Jim and Laura Burrows, Ben Turnbull and his wife Pat who run the pub, every one of them said, "*We're a small community and Louise was one of us.*" Every single one of them extols her virtues. Not a single one of them didn't like her, or at least will admit to not liking her. I know that people tend to canonise the dead and not say anything bad about them, but the wording, it's all too similar. Another popular one is, "*She threw herself into village life and became a part of our community.*" Then there's what they say about the Harmony House crowd. "*They were always acting strangely, creeping around. You'd come across them in the lanes or fields and they'd be intimidating.*" Anyone would think that they were trying to set them up as the fall guys.'

'Well, I'm sure that sixteen convicted criminals living close by could be intimidating to some.'

Harrison sighed.

'I'm not being blinkered, Dr Lane. I know that Harmony House is obvious but we have found evidence there that links us to Louise's death, quite apart from a second murder.'

Harrison chose his words carefully. 'We have to look at all scenarios, but in answer to your original question, no I don't think they were responsible for Louise's death. I think I know what the motive was, but I'm not quite there yet.'

'So why Finn Smith? You think that he found something out or was involved?'

'I'm less certain about Finn. I can't see the link yet, unless he found out that they were trying to frame them. Perhaps he caught someone breaking in that night and they had to silence him. Or simply that there needed to be a murder at the property for them to allow the police in so you could discover the planted evidence. For me, the latter is a strong possibility. You'd never have had enough grounds to be able to get a warrant to go into Harmony House without there being a murder reported and so you'd never have found the phone and other evidence.'

Gibbons shook his head. 'It's all possible, but that's all we seem to have right now: possibilities. We've sent it all for analysis – if there's any DNA or fingerprints then we'll find them.'

'Oi, what do you think you're doing?' An angry shout interrupted their conversation and a man came striding across the field from the direction of Nick Rogers's house. 'Who are you and what are you doing? Get out of here.'

Gibbons reached into his pocket and pulled out his police ID. 'Police, Mr—?'

The man visibly reduced his aggression and stepped back, but there was still a look of contempt on his features. 'Burrows. I work for Mr Rogers. We've had nonstop harassment from bloody press and those social media idiots.'

Harrison had already recognised Burrows from the TV interview, and there was another bell ringing in his memory too.

'What do you do for Mr Rogers?' Gibbons continued.

'I maintain the grounds and his garden.'

'Does that woodland belong to Mr Rogers?'

'No, it's common land that is.'

'Were you aware of a large pile of wood and garden waste that was in a clearing at the edge of those woods?'

Burrows hesitated. 'The dump pile, yes.' His aggression started to waver. 'I cleared it a few days ago. We do that every now and then, a service to the village you know, as it's where they dump their garden waste. Bloody miles to take it to the nearest green waste site.'

'I understand that pile had quite a bit of wood in it?'

'Wood? Not really. It was mostly grass cuttings and the like. I dug them into the ground and then flattened over.'

'No fence panels or chopped-down trees and branches?'

'Not really, maybe the odd bit.'

'Just the odd bit?'

Burrows gave a small nod and looked away from them, biting his lip.

'OK, Mr Burrows, thank you. I'm going to have some forensics officers here in a few minutes. We'd like access to that barn please.'

'The barn? Why?'

'I want to look at the equipment that's in there.'

'You'll have to get permission from the boss for that.'

'You can let him know, that's fine, but as I have reasonable cause to suspect that piece of machinery may have been involved in the murder of Louise Swift, I have just cause to examine it. Permission from the boss or not.'

'I'll go tell him.'

Burrows strode off back across the field.

'I'm going to have to start rattling a few cages,' Gibbons said to Harrison as they watched him. 'Care to join me in that task?'

'I'd be delighted.'

TWENTY-SEVEN

Harrison and DS Gibbons decided to get an answer on Charley Jones's whereabouts first. They both had concerns about her welfare, and there were more questions they both had about Louise's business tactics.

'She gave conflicting answers when we first spoke to her,' Harrison said to Gibbons as they walked up the street through the village. 'Either she knows what's gone on and her conscience is struggling, or she was actively involved.'

They stopped and knocked on the door of Charley Jones's house, stepping back and waiting for it to open. It didn't take long. Her mother, Anne, opened the door and smiled at the sight of them.

'Hello again, detectives, how can I help you?'

'We'd like to speak with Charley please, Mrs Jones.'

Neither man missed the smug look that appeared on Anne Jones's face. 'I'm afraid Charley is in South America. Gone travelling for a few months. I did tell one of your officers that yesterday.'

'Travelling in South America, since when? You didn't tell my officer that. You said she was with a friend.'

'She is with a friend. They left the day before yesterday. She'd been planning the trip for ages and as she'd lost her job she decided now was as good a time as any.'

'In the middle of a murder investigation?'

'You interviewed her, you took her statement. Nobody told us that she couldn't. Charley isn't a suspect you know. She was upset. She liked Louise. We thought it would do her good to get away from here with all this nonsense going on.'

And therein, thought Harrison, was the problem. It probably would be good for Charley to get away from the publicity, but that wasn't the real reason: Charley was the weakest link and someone wanted her out of the way.

'I think that's for me to say if Charley is a suspect or not, Mrs Jones, thank you. But, that's no problem, we can speak to Charley when she returns. When will that be?'

'I'm not entirely sure to be honest. She said she was going to go for about six months, or so but it might be longer if she's enjoying herself. You're only young once, detective, a year out is life-affirming for young people when they've finished their education.'

'That must be costing a few bob,' DS Gibbons added, no reaction to the news showing on his face.

Anne Jones's mouth thinned into a line of disdain. 'That's our business.'

'Could you give me Charley's mobile number please and also her flight details?'

'Of course, but she won't have her phone on very often. Roaming costs have shot up these days!'

Harrison's mobile started to buzz in his pocket and he excused himself from the conversation to answer it. He heard Anne Jones tell DS Gibbons her daughter's mobile number and what flight she had caught and knew full well that the DS was going to make sure Charley was alright and had made that flight. In this village, you could never be too careful.

'Alright, boss?' Ryan's voice came into his ear.

'Yes, how's things your end?'

'All good. Found out something interesting about one of your villagers. Jim Burrows took his wife's surname unusually, but maybe to escape his past. He was originally Jim Adebayo. Convicted murderer. Stabbed another teenager when he was just fifteen. I also think that he may have been living at Harmony House at one point. Can't one hundred per cent confirm that but—'

'Hang on,' said Harrison. He swiped his phone to look at his photographs. He'd taken one of the guest book at Harmony House, and there'd been more names in it than had been living there. Would Jim be on the list?

It didn't take him long to find the name.

'You're right, Ryan. He was there.'

'Cool. Might be worth having a chat with him then.'

'Oh yes indeedy, in fact we just met him. Thanks.'

'Boss, before you go. Are you aware that Nick Rogers was married?'

'Yes, he mentioned he'd been married. His wife took her own life.'

'Well, he would say that, but it's not necessarily the truth. He reckoned she'd been suicidal, but nobody knows what happened to her. She disappeared fifteen years ago!'

'Disappeared?'

'Yup, never found. But she was legally declared dead five years ago.'

'Don't suppose you know if it was her money or his that funds his lifestyle?'

'It's his so that wasn't a motive and she didn't have a big life policy. That was all looked into at the time. There's a sister who lives nearby. She never believed the suicide theory and still maintains that she was murdered.'

'Thanks for that, Ryan.'

When Harrison finished his call, he returned to Gibbons who was texting but looked up at him. 'Bloody travelling my arse. They've got her out the way, haven't they?'

'Looks that way.'

'I'm making sure she got on that plane,' Gibbons replied, 'and with a friend.'

Harrison relayed his conversation with Ryan to Gibbons.

'I was aware of the suicide theory and the investigation, but no blame was ever put on Rogers. She never used her phone or bank accounts again. The car was found near to a spot which is renowned for suicides.'

'Convenient.'

'Maybe, but we'll need something more concrete than the fact we aren't keen on the man, in order to reopen that investigation.'

Harrison sighed.

'I think the Burrows live next door to Louise Swift,' Gibbons said to him as they walked back down the street. 'Shall we see if Mrs Burrows is in first? Might catch her unawares. I really do want to up the pressure on these people.'

Mrs Burrows had just collected their daughter from nursery.

'It's not really that convenient,' she said to them, eyeing up DS Gibbons warily. 'I've literally just come in from work and picking up my daughter. Perhaps you can come back in an hour when my husband is here too?'

'Just a few minutes of your time.' Gibbons smiled charmingly at her and in order not to give her too much choice in the matter, started stepping through the door.

'In there,' she said, indicating a little sitting room. The cottage was a carbon copy of Louise Swift's apart from the decor. In the sitting room, a little girl was concentrating on dressing a doll.

'Who's this then?'

'This is Lilly.'

'Hi, Lilly.' DS Gibbons smiled and gave her a little wave. 'I remember when mine were that size, seems like only yesterday.'

While Gibbons was charming Lilly, Harrison had been looking at the photographs on their wall. Most of them were of Lilly, but there was also one of Laura and Jim at their wedding.

Harrison refocused his attention on Laura Burrows, just as DS Gibbons started asking his questions. 'So, Mrs Burrows, you live next door to Louise Swift.'

'Yes. Look I've spoken to police already. Given a statement.'

'I know. You didn't see or hear anything that night. You were both in all night and you liked Louise, that about right?'

'Yes.' She set her lips into a firm line, clearly not impressed with his response.

'Yes. The same as everyone else in the village has said.'

Laura Burrows shrugged.

'Did Louise ever do a reading for you, Mrs Burrows?'

She looked at him as though assessing what he had just asked her.

'She had a gift, you know,' she started, 'my mum died about eighteen months ago, she contacted her for me.'

Harrison noticed how Laura looked away after she'd said that, as though she didn't want to see their reaction to her words.

'Who do you think killed Louise?' DS Gibbons asked now.

Harrison could see where he was going with the line of questioning.

She shrugged. 'Probably that lot up at Harmony House. They're a bunch of weirdos.'

'But didn't your husband stay up at Harmony House for a while?'

Her eyes shot to DS Gibbons's face and her own features hardened further.

'Only for a short while, just so he could get back on his feet.

So? He told me what a bunch of lowlifes they are. He met me when he came into the village one day and I wasn't even allowed to visit him there, he had to sneak out to see me.'

'So he didn't like the place then? What about the other men, and Finn?'

'Finn was a judgemental, holier than thou type. You'd have thought he was some bloody religious messiah the way he'd talk about redemption. He didn't like Jim, kicked him out, but it did us both a favour. He came to live with me after that and...' She swept her arm towards Lilly.

'You say *was* judgemental?' DS Gibbons picked her up on her use of the past tense in relation to Finn.

'Yeah. I heard he'd been killed by one of his ex-con friends.'

'Who did you hear that from, Mrs Burrows?'

'It was on the news, wasn't it? I can't remember now.'

'We haven't released any names.'

Laura Burrows crossed her arms over her chest and stared back at DS Gibbons, then shrugged. She looked uncomfortable but stood her ground.

'Your husband works for Nick Rogers, doesn't he? Drives machinery?'

'He does his land maintenance. Nick's got fields and some woodland.'

'Is Jim a tree surgeon?' Harrison asked her.

'He's not one of them who climbs up trees, he calls someone in for that, but they've got an extending cradle thing so he can reach up high if needs be.'

'An extending cradle?' DS Gibbons clarified.

'Yeah, you know it's on like an arm and someone can stand in the basket. They use it at the house as well and it was used to do some roof repairs to one of the cottages once too.'

'And your husband was definitely here, at home with you and little Lilly on the night that Louise was killed?'

'Yes. I've told you that already. He didn't go out.'

'Well thank you, Mrs Burrows, you've been very helpful.'

'One final thing,' Harrison said as she was about to show them the door. 'Have you ever visited the Thistleford Community Church?'

'No. They're a little too OTT for my liking.'

'Are you aware that your husband helped them with the church renovations?' Harrison was aware of DS Gibbons looking at him.

'I was aware, detective,' Laura said to him, making the usual assumption that he too was a police officer. 'That was before Jim and I were married. He was looking for some meaning in his life after what happened at Harmony House. He doesn't go there or anything.'

'Thank you for your help.' Harrison smiled at her.

Mrs Burrows didn't look overly pleased and Harrison judged that she hoped she hadn't been too helpful at all.

Once they'd left her house, Gibbons turned to him.

'What's that about Jim Burrows and the church, you didn't tell me that?'

'No, because I didn't know either until two minutes ago. It was a hunch. I saw some machinery in one of the renovation photographs up there and wondered if maybe he'd helped out.'

'Sounds like he's a mixed-up fellow going from one group to another trying to find his meaning in life. I bloody hope they've not tried to move that machinery before the team get there.'

'Will it help us anyway?' Harrison asked him. 'At the end of the day, even if we can prove that it could possibly have been used to make that bonfire, how are we going to prove who drove it? Jim's DNA will be all over it anyway.'

'I know, I know, don't depress me. The only hope we do have is for something from Louise which can at least prove that the machinery was used that night. No evidence, no witnesses, but I'm not giving up yet,' DS Gibbons said. 'Let's go and see what Rogers has to say, see if he's been rattled at all.'

Gibbons's hope that Rogers was rattled was instantly dashed the second that he and Harrison arrived at Nick Rogers's house.

'Afternoon, gentlemen, come on in,' Rogers said, smiling at them and waving them into his house.

'I understand you wanted to look at the machinery we use in the grounds. I've told Burrows that's absolutely fine. He's a little jumpy after all those annoying TikTok people kept turning up and harassing us. How's the investigation into Louise's death going? I hear that one of those Harmony House men has been found dead. I knew it wouldn't be long before they started turning on each other.'

'Investigations are ongoing Mr Rogers.'

'Well anything that you require from me, please just ask.'

'Why is it that there's absolutely no CCTV at all, no smart doorbells, no phone footage, no car dashcams, nothing in this village whatsoever?'

Rogers overdramatised his look of shock at Gibbons's words. 'Well that's quite simple DS Gibbons, we like our privacy. Is there anything wrong with that? That's why this media and public intrusion into our lives has been so galling to all of us. We're all looking forward to this being sorted and for us being able to get on with our lives in peace.'

'Louise Swift can't get on with her life. She's dead,' Gibbons said pointedly.

'Yes. That's a sad truth, detective, but that is not my fault, or the fault of any of my community. We want to see whoever committed her murder brought to justice. Louise was a part of our village, a gifted young woman. She died for those gifts at the hands of somebody or a group of people who didn't appreciate her like we did.'

'What happened to all the wood in the dump pile in the trees, Mr Rogers?'

'Wood? I've no idea, detective. I suspect that the Harmony

House men took it. They were always skulking around picking up firewood wherever they could find it. I've no doubt also stealing other things too.'

'So why did you use your employee and machinery to clear that site?'

'Because I wanted to stop those men from coming around that's why. Is that a crime? I also have done it before to clear the garden waste that is deposited there. Why on earth are you asking me about that? What kind of crime do you think I've committed by helping my community?'

'You are aware that we are looking for the source of the wood that was used in the bonfire that killed Louise Swift. We have some evidence which shows that there was wood including fence panels and tree branches in that pile. We also have evidence that a vehicle, similar to the one you own, was used to prepare the bonfire.'

'Are you suggesting that someone took my vehicle and then wood from the dump pile to murder Louise? That's outrageous. How brazen.'

'I'm suggesting your machine was used to take wood and then your machine was used to erase any trace of the dump pile.'

Nick Rogers stared at DS Gibbons. 'I don't think I quite understand what you're getting at, detective. Isn't that what I just said? Do you have some evidence in relation to this matter that I should know about?'

The two men stared at each other for a few more moments. The air was thick with tension.

DS Gibbons smiled. 'I was just offering some suggestions as to what has been happening around here.'

Harrison took the moment to ask a question. 'Mr Rogers, I understand that your wife, Debbie, disappeared fifteen years ago and that you had her legally declared dead?'

'Yes. That's common knowledge, detective, what of it?'

'I'm not a detective, Mr Rogers, I'm a psychologist,' Harrison said. He noticed a slight tremor in Rogers's facial muscles when he said that. 'I was just wondering if Louise was able to get in contact with your wife for you?'

'She offered. I declined. It took me a long time to come to terms with my wife leaving me. She wasn't an easy woman to live with, bi-polar condition you know. I suspected right from the start that she'd almost certainly taken her own life, but of course the police weren't able to find any evidence of that, her body was never retrieved.'

'So, if you believe that Louise was so gifted, why did you not want to talk to your wife and ask her why she'd left? Get some answers? I know that would certainly be what I'd want to know.'

For the first time Nick Rogers seemed lost for words. 'I... Well, I just didn't want to. I didn't want to open up old wounds.'

'Interesting,' was all Harrison said.

Rogers's eyes darted between him and DS Gibbons, who gave another of his smiles.

'Thank you for your cooperation, Mr Rogers, that's all for now. I'm sure my team won't detain your vehicles long and then you can continue your community work.'

When they were well out of earshot and sight, Gibbons turned to Harrison and gave him a beaming smile.

'Well done. At least one of us managed to wipe that smarmy smile off his face. So, what's your thinking?'

'I was thinking he knows full well she's dead because he killed her. There's no photographs of her in their home, there was no emotion when I mentioned her. I know it's been fifteen years, but when someone you supposedly loved disappears like that, you keep a little flame burning somewhere for them, don't you?'

'Perhaps, or maybe his ego is just angry at her for daring to leave him, I can't imagine he was an easy man to have to live with. Either way, please don't foist another murder on me right now. I think we've got enough with trying to solve these two.'

'Oh I doubt we'd find a shred of evidence after all this time if he did kill her. He'd have disposed of her a long time ago.'

'And, if they don't find any evidence on those vehicles then I'm not sure where that leaves our current enquiries!' Gibbons said to Harrison. 'Let's get back to the station and see how the rest of the team are doing.'

It was in the car on the way to the station that Harrison's phone buzzed in his pocket. It was Ryan again.

On a roll. You're going to want to see this. Original was deleted, but someone shared it on some obscure psychic channel, Ryan's message read.

As Harrison watched and listened to the video that his assistant had sent, he realised he'd finally cracked the motive for Louise's murder. He just needed a little more information to corroborate his theory.

TWENTY-EIGHT

Ryan sent Harrison the address he needed and he was relieved to see it was only about thirty miles from Thistleford. He jumped on his bike and arrived at the neat suburban house a short while later. As Harrison walked down the path, the front door opened and a stylish middle-aged woman greeted him.

'Mrs Chester, thank you for agreeing to see me at such short notice.' He held out his hand and found a warm shake in return.

'I'm more than happy to talk about my sister, Dr Lane – no one really listened to me when she went missing. Please do come in. Are you OK with cats? We have two Siamese who might want to check you out.'

'I'm absolutely fine, thank you for asking,' he replied, following her into a sitting room which although a little chintzy for his tastes, was tidy and comfortable. Photographs of young children and teenagers lined the walls and bookcases, along with some other images of what he presumed to be older family members. Ellen Chester walked up to one particular photograph of a smiling blond woman, sitting atop a magnificent horse.

'This is Debbie, just after she'd got married to Nick. He was still treating her alright then and she was happy. Didn't last long,' she added disdainfully, handing the photograph to Harrison. 'Can I make you a tea or something?'

'A glass of water would be fine, thank you,' Harrison said, looking into the smiling face of the woman who'd been missing for fifteen years. He could see the resemblance between her and Ellen; there was no doubting they were sisters, but Ellen had carried on living while her sister had been frozen in time.

'Here you go,' Ellen said coming back into the room with a glass of cold water. 'So, you want to know about my sister's marriage to Nick?'

'If you don't mind. Have you kept in touch?'

Ellen sneered at the suggestion. 'The second that the police dropped the case and people stopped looking for Debbie, I never heard from him again. Can't say it wasn't good riddance. I was only ever polite to him for her sake.'

'He told us that Debbie suffered from depression, that she was bi-polar?'

'He made that up. She was never diagnosed as bi-polar and her so-called depression was all down to him. He was a controlling, egotistical bully. He stopped her from doing anything without him, didn't even like her coming to see me. She withdrew into herself.'

'And there were never any children?'

'At first she hoped there would be, but after a few months, she decided that their relationship wasn't tenable and she didn't want to bring a child into the world in those circumstances.'

'What do you think happened to your sister?'

Ellen took the photograph off Harrison and looked at it, tears rimming her eyes. 'I think he killed her. They were arguing a lot. She'd nearly called the police on him once before, but he'd apologised and she'd relented. This time she was really going to leave him. We'd talked about her coming to live with us for the first few days while she got sorted. She'd already brought some of her things over and all she had to do was jump. I'd spoken to her the day before and we were expecting her, only she never turned up. He said she'd walked out, driven off somewhere in one of her so-called dark moods. They found her car by one of the big lakes and put two and two together to make fifteen. I'm telling you there's no way she would have taken her own life, she was excited about starting again without Nick, and she was afraid of water, barely swam.' Ellen stopped talking, the words caught in her throat.

'I'm so sorry for your loss,' Harrison said to her gently. 'I'm afraid I don't think that I can offer you any justice after all this time.'

Ellen looked at him and gave a weak smile. 'I know. It's just good for her story to be told and if it helps stop him doing it to someone else, then it's justice of a kind for Debbie.'

Harrison left Ellen's home and rode back to the incident room with an uncomfortable feeling in the pit of his stomach. He'd always known that it was unlikely there'd be any justice for Debbie after all these years, but he feared there was going to be no justice for Louise or Finn either. Worse still, he was worried that the wrong person or people would pay for their deaths. He needed to share all that he'd gathered with DS Gibbons and the rest of the team, and hope that they'd see what he saw.

TWENTY-NINE

DS Gibbons gathered the team in the meeting room to hear what Harrison had to say and watch the video that Ryan had sent through to him. You wouldn't have seen a quieter room or greater concentration even if it had been the greatest Oscar-winning movie of all time.

Louise Swift and what looked like virtually the entire village were in the Thistleford Arms pub. Someone was clearly using a mobile phone to record her and she was holding what in theory was a cold reading, but no doubt she'd already researched well and primed herself with every villager's background. It wasn't the only video like this, there were others with her and the villagers which were still available online and indeed the people of Thistleford actively encouraged their sharing. This one though, was different.

'Someone here suffers from sore feet. They're embarrassed about it, but there's no need to be embarrassed. You can get help. Your guardian angel wants me to help you. You know who you are, come and see me.' Louise smiled around the room as though she didn't know who it was, but her eyes held on Jim Burrows.

'I have an older gentleman who wants their son to know that he shouldn't worry about his mother. He's watching over her and he'll be there for her.' Louise let her eyes rest on Mark O'Neil.

'There's also a nice lady here, an older lady who suffered at the end but wants her daughter to know that she's fine. She loves you very much. Is there someone here who is hurting?' Louise scanned the room. Laura Burrows tentatively held up her hand. 'Me, I lost my mum just a few weeks ago.'

'Ah, Laura, your mum is here, she can feel your pain and she wants you to be happy. She's happy. She's at peace now.'

Laura Burrows started sobbing and turned to her husband, burrowing her face into his shoulder.

Then Louise clutched her forehead and closed her eyes, swaying slightly. 'There's someone here. Someone angry. They were sent to the other side before their time and they want me to tell their story.' She clutched at her chest. 'Oh, it's somebody who should have loved them and protected them but instead they hurt her.' Again, she opened her eyes and scanned the room, but this time Harrison noticed she stayed staring at Nick Rogers a moment longer than anyone else.

Harrison stopped the video and turned to look at the sea of expectant faces.

'She's good, isn't she?'

Heads nodded and people murmured in agreement.

'They thought so. The people of Thistleford embraced Louise Swift. They truly believed she was gifted and she strung them along for nearly two years, taking their money, peddling lies, fake medicines, and I think in Nick Rogers's case, eventually blackmailing him.'

Harrison brought up an image of the photograph that Ellen had shown him earlier, that he'd taken on his phone.

'This is Debbie Rogers, his wife who disappeared fifteen years ago. The police investigation at the time found they'd had a tempestuous relationship. She'd been to the doctors once before with bruising that was felt to indicate domestic violence and yet they couldn't find anything to incriminate him when she disappeared. Her body has never been found and she was legally declared dead. He may have got away with the perfect murder and that's why when Louise said what she did that night, he might have started to panic. Was she really talking to his dead wife? Even if you don't fully believe in all this, the doubt could have been enough for him to give himself away to Louise. For him to fear that she really knew he'd killed his wife, that somehow she'd found something out.

'He told us she was bi-polar and difficult to live with. Her sister tells a very different story and I've checked her medical records, Debbie was never diagnosed as bi-polar. The closest she got was being prescribed some pills for depression. What we do know is that Louise lived rent free for several months due, according to Nick Rogers, to cash flow problems, but her bank balance was more than healthy.'

'I can't believe that he would really believe that she was speaking to his dead wife!' one of the officers spoke up. 'He strikes me as a pretty down to earth sort.'

'People like Louise prey on our insecurities. Psychic fraud is on the increase. There have been some huge cases involving millions of pounds and global crime rings. Then there are just individuals like Louise who prey on vulnerable people. I don't mean those who might be vulnerable people, easily taken in, I'm talking about professional intelligent people who are just human and want to believe in something.'

'So if she's not the real deal, how does she know this stuff? How could she look at someone and know they have a problem or that they've lost a relative or killed one?' The same officer asked.

'In this case, it's what they call a warm reading. She knew exactly who the villagers were. She'd lived among them, gathering evidence, and she'd obviously done her research on them. She was a clever woman, an astute people watcher who no doubt collected information over the course of a few weeks before she started to wow them with her gift. She probably tested out her theories before the big reveal, piecing together information about every one of them.

'I found newspapers in her office where she'd highlighted the names of widows and widowers in the funeral listings. I have no doubt that she'd have regularly approached a few of them to say she could connect with their deceased partner, just like she did with Mrs Wilson who she went to see the day before she died. She would pretend to randomly bump into them in the street and then come out with something that made them think she was really talking to their loved one. It's a common tactic and the victim is desperate to believe it's true.'

'So she was just a con artist?'

'Not just any kind of con artist. Louise Swift was a mentalist.'

'A what? She had a mental health problem?'

'No.' Harrison almost smiled at the totally bemused expression on the detective's face.

'Mentalism is effectively a performance whereby the mentalist appears to be a mind reader, or in Louise's case, a spiritual reader, but is in fact using well-honed magical tricks, sleights of hand, and psychological illusions to fool you. Derren Brown is probably the most famous proponent of this technique at the moment, and there's also Banachek and Uri Geller. It's absolutely mesmerising when you see someone who is skilled performing. Louise Swift might not have been in the same league as Derren Brown but she was good and she combined that with her excellent ability to watch people and figure out what they were thinking. I use some of the techniques she would have used whenever I'm interviewing someone, or watching someone being interviewed. We all do it to a greater or lesser degree. Focusing on body language, subtle gestures and how their body is reacting, such as sweating or anxiety when I say things or how they give their replies. The little telltale signs can be far more revealing than any answers they tell me.'

'But I thought you said she also did her tarot readings on TikTok, wouldn't that mean she's not able to respond to people or know anything about them?' DS Gibbons asked.

'She did, but she used a fishing technique to get her clients hooked. Her ability to spin a good story and be persuasive pulled people into connecting with her one-on-one and even on video she'd be able to detect when she was on a good topic. It's actually quite simple if you have the confidence to do it. She knew how to start with general comments, based around the kinds of challenges everyone has at different times of their lives. You know the usual: relationships, money, grief. She'd say that if you were watching her video then it was meant for you. Nine times out of ten or maybe a lot more, people would have scrolled past, but every now and then she'd strike lucky. Somebody who'd just broken up with their partner, or who was feeling lonely, or broke, or had lost someone close to them, would catch her video and it would resonate with them. No matter how unlikely and ridiculous it might seem, that person's torment would mean they grasped at the hope she offered.

'Most of us seek some kind of guidance, we look for signs when we're having a bad time that our luck will change, whether that's two magpies, angel numbers, touching wood for luck, tarot cards, crystals or seeking solace from more formal religions. But it's easy money to prey on peoples' insecurities and offer hope to them. Unfortunately, it's usually false hope but if you keep on saying things will change, that someone will come along, then eventually they might, just because of the odds that at some point they would have anyway – and then you can say you predicted that.'

'What about when she had to do readings that weren't

warm, when she didn't know who she was going to be talking to? I've seen videos of her doing these things live, how could she fool people then?'

'She'd start throwing information at the person she was reading for until they began to indicate that she was onto something, and then gradually she honed in on a relative or friend or relationship that the person was concerned about by feeding off their reactions and the information they gave back. She would make a big fuss about these successes and bury any less successful attempts she'd made that hadn't hit home, so that when she finished with the person, they'd have felt as though she'd totally got them.'

Harrison paused and looked at the faces in the room, some were shaking their heads, not because they disagreed with him but because they were disappointed. He wondered if any of them had fallen prey to someone like Louise in the past. As he expected, he got the next inevitable question.

'So are all of these psychics con artists?'

'I wouldn't say that, no. Some people really believe they're helping others and truly think they can convene with spirits. I've yet to meet someone who can persuade me they are genuinely speaking to the dead, but that's not to say that it's impossible. We have to have open minds. But if they're taking lots of money off people, especially when they know they're vulnerable, then I don't think they are helping; I'd question their motivations. Rather than getting someone to rely on them for some kind of validation and keeping on taking their money, what would be more beneficial to that individual would be to persuade people to help themselves – not rely on some external force to bring them good luck.'

'So how does all this connect to witchcraft and how she died?' Gibbons asked Harrison.

'It can seem like witchcraft to some people. Believe me, even experts get fooled. There was a famous paranormal experiment, Project Alpha in the late 1970s, when two young men were tested by scientists and appeared to exhibit paranormal powers. In fact they were using mentalism and magic tricks. One of those young men later went on to become the performer, Banachek.'

'Right, so she gets the villagers to believe she has these amazing powers, they think she's fabulous, so who is it that burnt her at the stake. Nick Rogers because he thought he'd been rumbled?' Gibbons asked, brow lined with furrows.

'All of them,' Harrison replied. 'Because the real motive for all the good folk of Thistleford was shame and embarrassment. It's collective narcissism. They thought they were better than everyone else. Nick Rogers curated these people. He owns almost all the cottages and so he chose who could live there. That gives him a hold over them and it also makes them all feel special. Chosen ones. In short they feel they deserve respect and are different to everyone else. They welcomed Louise into their group and she seemed to become one of them, until they found out she was actually conning them. Nick himself is the textbook case study of grandiose narcissism. He is not a man who would like to think he'd been duped.

'It's why so many victims of psychic fraud or even dating and financial fraud, don't come forward to the police and report the crimes. They're embarrassed. They are taken advantage of and by the time they realise what's going on they've usually lost a lot of money. In the villagers' cases, they believed in Louise. They told everyone how amazing she was. They drank her potions, said how she was curing their pain when in fact all she was doing was adding paracetamol to some herbs. Forensics have confirmed that's what the white powder traces were that we found in her pestle and mortar.'

'So how did they change their minds about her, to go from singing her praises to stoning and burning her to death?'

'I think it all really unravelled for her when Charley Jones went to work with her. Suddenly, Charley saw that it was all a sham and no doubt word soon got out that she'd played them like idiots. It was a huge miscalculation by Louise. They wanted to get their revenge, but they couldn't just kill her because then it would all come out that she'd been a con artist and they'd been idiotic enough to believe it all for so long. So, they made her out to be even more of a gifted psychic and came up with a scenario that it was some kind of religious killing, because she was a genuine witch who had to be burnt at the stake. That way, their reputations would be preserved because hers was.'

'How can you be so sure about this?'

'Let me show you this video that Louise put onto TikTok in which she does a tour of the lounge where she did personal readings and séances.' Harrison turned the video on but kept the sound on mute. 'On her bookshelf I spotted some books about mentalism. I also saw these...' He pointed at the screen. 'They're called spirit slates and are effectively magic tricks that psychics use to make it look like they are talking to the dead. When we went in there after Louise's murder, they'd disappeared along with her laptop, which would have no doubt had all her research on it. There were other tricks as well, such as the fan under the table and the specially folded pieces of paper she'd have got people to write on. The villagers didn't want anyone finding the proof that she wasn't gifted but was a scammer, and so they took it.

'For me, the indications that this wasn't a group of people who truly believed Louise to be a witch, were there right from the start. The signs that were spray painted on the walls in the cottage were what somebody who didn't understand or know witchcraft would have done. They weren't what people who truly believed her to be a witch and wanted to protect and cleanse the place would have left. It was a crude attempt to make it look as though there was a religious motive to her murder.'

'So where does Harmony House fit into all this? And the murder of Finn Smith, is that unconnected?'

'Harmony House is totally unconnected but they were the easy and most obvious scapegoats. Who was more likely to murder a woman like that: a bunch of convicted criminals who locked themselves away from society in some big country estate, or the respectable members of a village who adored Louise and had made her one of their own? The fact they all seemed to be happy up there in their big house, might have also rankled at the collective narcissistic traits of the villagers. Finn was a man with charisma and presence, Nick Rogers is just a bully.'

'So you think Nick killed Finn?'

'No. He wouldn't get his hands dirty like that. Jim Burrows, formerly Jim Adebayo, is an ex con, who lived at Harmony House for a while, but he didn't fit in. He didn't buy into their ethos and I suspect that Finn saw through him and asked him to leave. That no doubt rankled him. He wanted to ruin their idyll and so when his boss said they needed a scape goat, Harmony House was an easy fit. His wife told us herself that he used to sneak in and out of the place to go and visit her so it would have been easy for him to do the same to plant the evidence. I found signs that some kind of metal hooks, possibly from a rope ladder, had been used on the top coping stones near to the walled garden. There was also clear evidence on the ground outside that somebody had gone over that wall.'

'And I'd told Nick Rogers that we couldn't get into Harmony House because we had no reasons or evidence to be able to get a search warrant! I effectively signed Finn's death warrant!' DS Gibbons shook his head sadly.

Harrison raised his eyebrows and nodded slowly. 'That's what I think happened. Burrows didn't like Finn, he'd have been happy to get his revenge, sanctioned by his boss. I'd hazard a guess that knowing full well that Finn liked to get some fresh herbs each night for a bedtime drink, he timed it when everyone else was asleep, planted Louise's mobile phone in the fire, and killed Finn, betting on the fact that the men would report his murder to us and we would legally have a right to enter. The truth of the matter is that Louise's murder wasn't a ritualistic crime. Her death and that of Finn, were two revenge killings, one based on shame and the other on necessity.'

Harrison stopped and looked at the room full of faces who were staring at him.

'Wow,' DS Gibbons said, voicing what everyone else was no doubt thinking. 'So the Thistleford Community Church have nothing to do with any of this?'

'No, I don't think so. It's bordering on being a cult and their extreme views are not in line with today's moral and politically correct world view, so I'd be keeping a close eye on them. Pastor Sam could be a dangerous character – but to those under his control, not outsiders. Nick Rogers doesn't like them. Their presence and the fact they're using the Thistleford name irks him, so he has been happy that some suspicion has fallen on them and no doubt encouraged it in the hope of driving them away.'

'I totally follow what you're saying,' Gibbons continued. 'The motives and chain of events, and it would explain how the whole village could have easily built that bonfire overnight, but where's the evidence for all this, other than circumstantial?'

'That I'm afraid,' Harrison replied, 'is the challenge.'

THIRTY

'Thank you for your help.' DS Gibbons shook Harrison's hand as he prepared to leave. Harrison had written up his report and there was nothing further he could do in Thistleford. There were new cases coming in and he had to return to London. He was also eager to get back and see how Tanya was. She'd barely spoken to him since she'd left, just a few courtesy texts.

'Sorry I'm not leaving with people arrested and charged,' Harrison said to DS Gibbons.

'That's my job. You've debunked the witchcraft element and given us motive. I've got to find some evidence to prove it. We've already found out that the weather conditions that night meant there was no way that they wouldn't have smelt the bonfire smoke in the village. Neither was there any way that Nick Rogers or even Burrows wouldn't have heard that machinery being moved. They all saw and heard what went on and no doubt most, if not all of them, helped build that bonfire. We reckon that with just a dozen of them it would have only taken them around two or three hours.'

'You may have a chance with Charley Jones, but I suspect that by the time she's been away a while, she'd have grown stronger and telling the lies like all the rest of them, will come easier. What are you going to do about Harmony House?'

'The bag with the spray can and diesel in won't be enough for a charge either, it would be easy for them to argue that it had been planted. The mobile and laptop are harder to explain away, but again, with evidence that someone went over that wall, we can't prove who put them there.'

'And Finn's death?'

'Again, no new evidence so far. We'll keep both cases open and keep investigating. I'd still like to know where Finn got his money from originally.'

'Have you asked them?'

'No, I suppose I could give that a go.' DS Gibbons smiled at him.

Harrison set off for London on his bike, relieved to be getting away from the toxic atmosphere in Thistleford. It may have looked idyllic, but it was anything but. Who said the city was a dangerous place to live? Violence and hatred exist anywhere that people are found, no matter how beautiful the surroundings.

He had just left the town, when he saw Maggot and one of the other men cycling in with a cart of vegetables. Harrison turned and pulled over to say goodbye.

'I'm heading back to London, I've done all I can here, but I wish you all the best of luck.' He meant it. He may not have believed in Thistleford's idyll, but he did believe in Finn's Harmony House. Everyone deserved a second chance at life and if it meant society would also benefit, then it was a win-win.

'Cheers. If you're going back home does that mean you've solved the case? Are we going to be left alone again now?'

'We believe that we know who murdered Louise, and have

some strong suspicions as to who might have killed Finn too, but DS Gibbons is still working on gathering evidence.'

Maggot nodded solemnly. 'What they did to her wasn't right. They make out that they're nice people but they're not. Nobody should have had to suffer like she did.'

Harrison looked at the man. He was no fool. They knew what the villagers had done.

'Did Finn guess who was behind it?'

Maggot nodded again.

'And did he ever confront anyone about it?'

'He wanted to, but he also knew how vulnerable we were. It could have come back to bite us – like it very nearly did. We're a house of criminals living near to the site of a murder, it wasn't hard to guess who'd get blamed. Finn was passionate about Harmony House and what he'd achieved with it. He had so many more plans to expand it and didn't want to risk all our futures. Having to make that choice made him sad, but he chose Harmony House.'

'Can I ask you one more question?' Harrison said to him.

'If I can ask you one.'

'OK. How did Finn get his money?'

Maggot smiled. 'Euromillions. One of the first really big winners. Won it a couple of weeks after coming out of the nick. He never felt like he deserved it after the guy died during the burglary. Gave his family a million pounds, but he always said it wasn't anywhere near enough, that it would never bring him back to them. He wanted to do good with the money, you know? Thought if he could stop people like him from being pushed back into crime, then he was repaying at least some of his debt. Atoning for what he'd done.'

Harrison smiled sadly and nodded.

'My turn,' Maggot said, eyes narrowing. 'Do you think it was Jim who killed Finn?'

'You know I can't tell you that,' Harrison replied, feeling the penetrating gaze of the man's dark eyes.

'They'll never find enough evidence to convict him, will they?' Maggot continued. 'You don't have to tell me. You didn't deny it so that's my answer. He knew our routines and he knew how to get in and out. He hated Finn because Finn had seen him for what he was. I've also seen how the justice system works. I got away with stuff I shouldn't have, I saw others get hit harder than they should for making a mistake, and I've seen my fair share of those who seem respectable getting away with far worse than most of those blokes back at Harmony House, just because they looked or spoke like they couldn't possibly be criminals. Money and status gets you a long way and pays for some shit hot lawyers. Jim is part of them now, Nick Rogers will protect him because he has to.' Maggot paused and seemed to reflect on what he'd just said before looking back at Harrison.

'What are you all going to do without Finn?' Harrison asked him.

'Honour his legacy and ensure Harmony House continues as he intended it to. We all feel the same. We'll pull together and carry on – he had such great plans for the place.'

'That's good, I'm pleased you'll keep it going.'

'Yeah, well, we'd better get on. We need to get this fresh veg to the shop. Goodbye, Dr Lane.'

THIRTY-ONE

It was three weeks later, when Harrison was knee deep in mud looking at some ritualistic symbols carved into trees around a lake, that he got the phone call from DS Gibbons.

'Dr Lane, I hope I've not caught you at an awkward time?'

'You're fine, what can I do for you?'

'I just wanted to let you know that there's been a further development in the Thistleford case. Not a positive one I hasten to add. Both Nick Rogers and Jim Burrows have disappeared.'

'Disappeared?'

'Yes.'

'Are you suspecting that something has happened to them or that they've left the country?'

'We are concerned for them. Jim told his wife that he was meeting Nick and never returned home. Nick left the lights on at his house and a half-eaten meal behind.'

'And I suppose that as there's no CCTV anywhere around the village, you're struggling to know what's happened to them.'

'Correct. It seems Mr Rogers's need for privacy has not done him any favours.'

'I see.'

'Not expecting you to have any ideas on it, just thought you might like to know,' Gibbons said to him.

When Harrison ended the call, he didn't immediately go back to looking at the symbols. For a few moments he stood, looking out over the lake, thinking about Debbie Rogers, Louise Swift, and Finn Smith. The men at Harmony House turned their backs on crime, but they clearly hadn't been able to turn their backs on justice. If the law couldn't give it to them, he strongly suspected that they'd felt duty bound to serve it themselves.

A fish breached the water and made a splash just a few feet away. He'd seen a kingfisher earlier and that was no doubt keeping a close eye out but was too wary to come close to where Harrison stood. As his mind wandered, he thought about Tanya and the difficult conversation they'd had when he'd returned to London. She wanted more from him than he felt he could give right now. He wasn't sure if that was a temporary situation, in part brought on by the tsunami of emotion and memories that Pastor Sam and the atmosphere at the Community Church had invoked in him, or if it was something more permanent. One thing he did know was that he had to keep on with the hunt for his mother's killer and he could never turn his back on his work. His fear was that those two reasons might never go away. That he might never be able to fully commit and that wasn't fair to Tanya. They'd gone out for dinner and agreed to take a step back for a couple of weeks, see how they both felt after some time apart. That was two weeks ago, and they were due to meet up again tonight. He really wasn't sure if he was ready for that conversation again.

Harrison took a few deep breaths and looked at nature all around him, pastel colours in the pale afternoon sun, beautiful and raw. Society seems to rise above the laws of nature, shunning the harsh and the brutal, and putting on a show of polite culture... or does it? Every day he saw the results of those who practised rituals, believed in superstitions, or craved notoriety through an abhorrent act that they hoped to blame on their beliefs. But in the end, it wasn't some external evil force that had driven them to it, but the corruption within themselves.

The people of Thistleford had behaved like a pack of wild animals turning on the outsider and instead of seeking out the justice they could have received through the courts, meted out their own brand of revenge in order to save face. It seemed only fitting therefore that the two who had the largest parts to play in the deaths of Louise, Finn and Debbie, should also receive their punishment in the raw.

But that wasn't for Harrison to judge.

He returned his attention to the symbols and thought about the state of the mind that had carved them into the bark of the majestic trees around him.

A LETTER FROM THE AUTHOR

Dear reader,

Many thanks for coming this far on Harrison's journey, I hope you have enjoyed his ninth investigation.

If you would like to hear about my new releases, offers, and get a FREE novella telling the story of Harrison's first case in the Ritualistic Behavioural Crime unit, then you can sign up to my readers' club at www.gwynbennett.com.

You can also sign up to get the latest updates on my new releases with Storm Publishing:

www.stormpublishing.co/gwyn-bennett

I'd also really appreciate it if you could leave a review on whichever platform you consumed this story on, and join in the conversation on mine and Storm's social media pages.

Thank you so much!

The inspiration behind this story came from several areas. The first was scrolling through TikTok and seeing the endless videos of people who promise that they can read my fortune and help me with a host of life's problems (I wish!). Like Harrison, I'm not a total non-believer, I'm open-minded but my only experience so far of a clairvoyant was disappointing. (Having said that I still say good morning to single magpies and touch wood for luck!)

Like many, I have also been transfixed by the terrible witch hunts of the seventeenth century, when so many innocent people were tortured and put to death because an individual or community deemed them to be 'different', dangerous or just for revenge.

The third inspiration was watching the world's top mentalists, like Derren Brown, perform. They seem to defy logic with their amazing skills that for all the world look like magic and sorcery, but of course are just well-practised talent. Louise's fate became the culmination of all these inspirations.

Thank you again for taking the time to read my book. Without you, Harrison Lane would just be stuck inside my head instead of living and breathing on the pages.

Happy reading and please do keep in contact.

Best wishes

Gwyn Bennett

facebook.com/GwynGBwriter

x.com/GwynGB

instagram.com/gwyngb

amazon.com/author/gwynbennett

bookbub.com/authors/gwyn-bennett

ACKNOWLEDGEMENTS

A big thank you to the whole team at Storm who have helped bring this book to you. In particular, Kathryn Taussig, my publisher, Natasha Hodgson and Shirley Khan for their editing and proofreading, and Tash Webber for the fabulous cover. There's also the brilliant George Weightman, who narrates the audio books.

Printed in Great Britain
by Amazon